Anatomy
of a
Vampire

Anatomy of a Vampire

of a

1912

John Matthias

PALMETTO
PUBLISHING
Charleston, SC
www.PalmettoPublishing.com

Hardcover ISBN: 979-8-8229-6657-4
Paperback ISBN: 979-8-8229-6658-1
eBook ISBN: 979-8-8229-6659-8

The journal of
Dr. A Lucard
1912

a frightening summer
of sensually vague memories

Table of Contents

The vampires of our imagination have never been observed, but what if they did exist? All the evidence we have on them is based upon a murky past, eyewitness accounts, and possible victims. The following is a body of conjectures and assumptions based upon what we have to rely upon from a scientific perspective, not the superstitious one that stipulates vampires as being the bloodsucking supernatural undead who prey upon sleeping virgins. This belief falls outside the realm of this study and is a matter of faith, which can be debated in other forums. I'm saying that the supernatural identity attributed to vampires may have alternative scientific explanations, some explained herein.

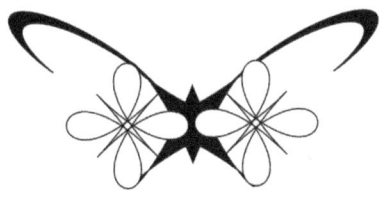

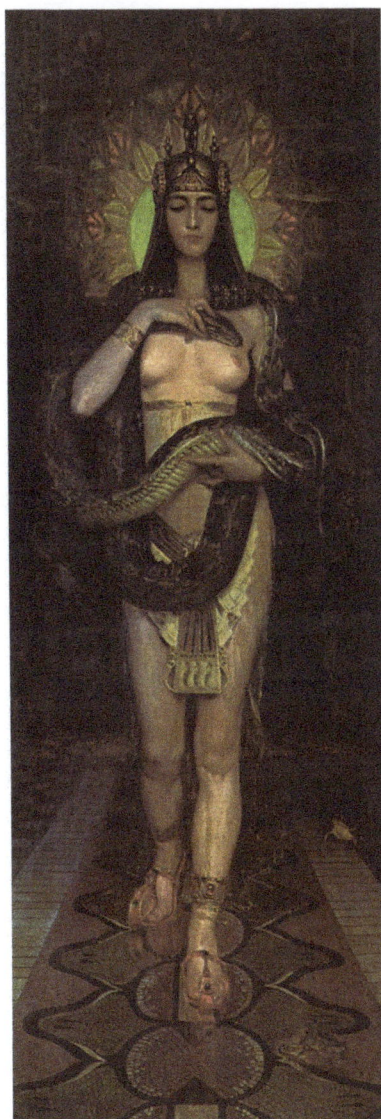

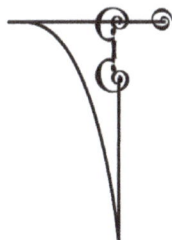

"You see things and you say, why? But I dream things that never were and I say why not!"

George Bernard Shaw

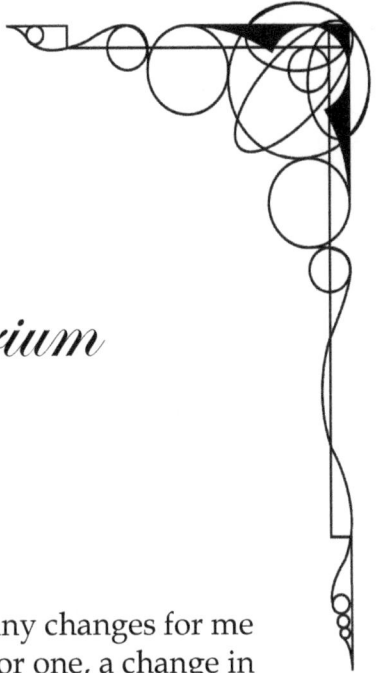

1 - Delirium

September brought many changes for me as a boy growing up in Dublin. For one, a change in season, though, in reality, there is only one in Ireland, and it can more accurately be described as the four stages of winter and not the four seasons that the rest of the world seems to enjoy. School also began again that month, dreaded amongst Irish youth because of how these Catholic institutions harshly instilled education, but for me, there was a greater fear: flu season. It always struck me in September, and it came as clockwork as the month itself. These microbes always wreaked havoc on my system for some reason, like I was a cursed mortal, the target of angry gods. High fevers were the stage for the most horrifying and lucid hallucinations. Once out of my school years, these annual bouts eventually ceased visiting me. I mention this only because I know the power of hallucinations on the conscious being. The mind is powerful enough to invent a sense of reality that even the eyes are fooled into believing; as if by some magic, the eye becomes a reverse projector, no longer submitting information to the brain, which is what gives us a sense of the tangible world, but projecting intangible creations from the brain. Something that is as real as reality itself if it is seen by the individual; how can one possibly convince him otherwise? This, indeed, is a premise for philosophical arguments as to how reality is actually defined.

I'm relaying this only due to the strangest events I encountered over the summer of 1912. I have set to recording them while they are yet still fresh in my mind, or at least as vivid as I can recall. Much of what I do recall still stifles me; it is vague, hazy, and confusing, but recorded more for my own sanity than for any other audience. It has caused me to reflect on the thin line that separates reality from the imagination, or as I would rather define it, the world outside and the one within.

Please excuse me; you do not know of me, so allow me first to introduce myself. My name is Ariel Lucard, and I teach the natural sciences at Trinity College in Dublin, or I did until recently — my post has since been without me. Do not be misled by my name, which exposes an Eastern ancestry but only on one side of the family. I am as Irish as any other Irishman, and my family has lived here for more generations than I care to recount. I am currently recovering in the Rotunda Hospital and have been here for almost three months now, suffering from a sickness that has doctors vexed.

Each day, I feel myself getting stronger, but

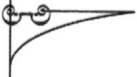

the first two months here, I cannot recall. Delirium, cold sweats, and fevers were tempered with heavy sedatives, leaving me in a twilight world that knew not time nor rational thought. I feel strange, not quite myself sometimes; surges run through my body on vascular highways. Last night I asked the nurse to turn off the light, but the only light on was a half-moon in a clouded sky. The sound of water being poured into a glass has the thunder of Victoria Falls. Perhaps it's the drugs and long bouts of rest causing hyperactivity, perhaps not. What is wrong with me? What got me here is the subject of this journal, so I should start at its beginning. I am hoping what is held within incites at least some curiosity so as to prompt further research, but I also understand those who would reject such an invitation out of fear, for great discoveries often come at a price of uneven worth.

It was about two days before breaking for the Christmas holidays last December, and I was leaving the lecture room when I was approached by a woman in black. Her frame was slight, her face soft but with a great sadness in her eyes. She knew me by name and introduced herself as Mrs. Kelly, Dr. Edward Kelly's wife.

I had studied under Dr. Kelly at Dublin University and had known he had gone missing some years ago. A little embarrassed, I could not look her in the eye as I had never paid my condolences. I was young at that time, with my head on other things. My first words were, "Sorry to have heard about your husband. Please forgive me for not sending my regrets." I was just about to justify my reason when I

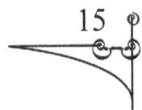

17th of July 1898

Dearest Jane

I don't have much time, so this will be brief. As a scientist, I was forever skeptical; for the longest time, I had ignored the symptoms and pushed aside the evidence. Research has landed me here for the sake of providing you with a better life. But man's curiosity is sometimes stupidity. Now I fear—I fear because I do believe. We are not alone but have an adversary, one of greater intelligence, ingeniously designed, with greater strengths than ours but few of our frailties.

I am writing this from the land beyond the forest, or, as most would call it, Transylvania. I feel a dread upon me that I may not return, for here I am, no longer sapient, no longer at the apex of the food chain. If the wolves and serpents don't seize me, there is a creature who certainly will. Give the children all my love.

Forever yours in love

Edward

thought it best not to; I had no real excuse other than being self-absorbed in my academic pursuits.

Dr. Kelly had gone missing in Romania fourteen years ago. He was a sickly man on a physical level but with a brilliant mind. I recall he had been commissioned by a wealthy foreign dignitary to lead a privately funded research mission in the Carpathian Mountains of Romania. No further details were ever dispensed beyond this. Normally, he would never have taken such a commission, but the purse was attractive enough to give his wife and four children some security in life in the event his ailment would prematurely disable him. He was no doubt more aware of his sickness than the medical profession could diagnose. The assignment was only to last the summer months between school terms before he'd return; he never did. The fact that the incident took place on foreign soil left police here at a loss, nor was much word ever received from investigators in Romania as to his whereabouts. I was inquiring as to whether she had heard anything of the case since then when she handed me a letter.

Though written back then, she had only received it a fortnight ago. It was from her husband. The letter appeared to have been written in haste and in a cold way, quite contrary to his normal warm manner when corresponding with his wife, but the handwriting was his. With no one else to turn to, she had turned to me, whom she knew through her husband's words. I wasn't in any way the best student of Dr. Kelly's class, but he had always appreciated the thoroughness of my research in

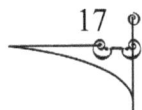

study. I was an avid reader, which, in some ways, compensated for my shortcomings when it came to competing against brighter students. I told Mrs. Kelly I'd look into the matter over the holidays but didn't guarantee anything. The mysterious source who had commissioned the investigation was gracious enough to forward Dr. Kelly's payment in full, with extra to Mrs. Kelly perhaps out of some guilt, even though Dr. Kelly was only halfway through his research when he disappeared.

Dr. Kelly, I found out, had been sent to Romania to research the vampire myth, but with an urgency that defied this explanation. It was also a subject outside of his field, Paleoanthropology being his specialty. Over the holidays, I began researching a subject I knew absolutely nothing about; even with the great success of *Dracula*, written by one of my own countrymen, I had not read the novel. Fiction simply didn't interest me; the pursuit of facts and science did. January saw me return to class, leaving aside my research into history and Eastern folklore on Dracula. There was not a lot of information found on either subject within the walls of Trinity Library, which housed the most extensive collection of books in Ireland, and since it wasn't a subject that completely enraptured me, it was forgotten about within a matter of weeks as I became consumed once again by my work.

On an unusually bright sunny day in February, I received a package delivered to the university and into my hand by courier, for which I had to sign. The package was a leather-bound satchel, and an off-white card accompanied it, which was handed to me first. The card was from a Mr. Stefanistsa; it was blunt but formal, with a brief introduction followed by an acknowledgment of who I was and then straight to the point with an offer to continue the work Dr. Kelly had left off with. The offer sold itself based on the financial compensation alone, in words I didn't doubt based upon its presentation, obviously from a person of wealth and nobility. I could only assume he knew of me through Mrs. Kelly's visit, but he also seemed aware of my qualifications and field of study. Within the satchel were clippings, notes, and reports concerning recent events throughout Europe, but these were events I found hard to believe, let alone investigate. I believed it all to be a hoax or simply ignorance that could be explained scientifically. Riches were not a pursuit of mine, though they would certainly aid me in my research, but the assignment was ridiculous. I couldn't accept it.

I was inventing my refusal of this generous offer, toying with the words in my mind as I got home that evening. On reaching my door, however, I found there a large crate approximately two feet square; in it were books. I spent the evening skimming and skipping through them. Many were books probably not available in Ireland; some were histories, some metaphysical, others religious, most likely acquired in London since they were in English. Many, however, were obvious translations from other languages based on the horrendous spelling and grammar mistakes. Others appeared very old, quite possibly collectibles, if not for reading, then surely mantelpiece ornaments,

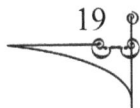

THE ILLUSTRATED LONDON NEWS

No.   —VOL. 7.]   FOR THE WEEK ENDING SATURDAY, FEBRUARY 9, 1856.   [SIXPENCE

The *Illustrated London News* reported on a strange incident in 1856. One source disclosed that "workmen laboring in a tunnel for a railway line, between Saint-Dizier and Nancy, in France, were cutting through Jurassic limestone when a large creature stumbled out from inside it. It fluttered its wings, made a croaking noise, and dropped dead. According to the workers, the creature had a 10-foot wingspan, four legs joined by a membrane, black leathery skin, talons for feet, and a toothed mouth. A local student of paleontology identified the animal as a pterodactyl. The report had the animal turn to dust, as soon as it had died."

Note: Since the creature was said to have turned to dust, the truthfulness of this reported story could not be validated. However, if one is to assume it is true, then perhaps it was not a pterodactyl. Other creatures, based upon the conjectures of this journal, would also fit the description (this assumption was not included in the above article).

lavishly decorative and of great aesthetic beauty. This man was going to great lengths to persuade me; why?

One of the clippings was from the *Illustrated London News*, a newspaper of credible reputation. I wrote to the paper's editor seeking validation of the clipping. Eventually, after a few weeks, he responded in the affirmative: the article was real. And so I took to researching the new material supplied, noting and jotting down bits and pieces as I saw fit. Before long I found myself bound to the subject matter. Books of foreign antiquity gave me new insight into other cultures, clothing my dreams with exotic ambiance.

One collection of writings that caught my attention was by Helena Blavatsky. Her work was a dense compilation of theosophical writings, most of which I was too ignorant to comprehend and too irreligious to care about. Ms. Blavatsky wrote with a very persuasive tone, and her book offered many insights into vampirism, even dating back to Proclus. I was curious as to the source material she had access to. She was said to be very well-traveled, and in my attempts to contact her, I found that she had passed away some years previous. However, I was turned on to Mrs. Annie Wood Besant, who had replaced her as the society's President: Ms. Wood, as she preferred to be addressed. I was able to correspond with her but unable to meet her, as much of her time was spent in India. She was likewise a prolific writer with an extensive knowledge of religion and metaphysics. However, she filled my head with more information than I cared to assimilate and had a tendency to go off on tangents I didn't care to pursue. She likewise

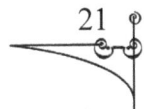

pointed me in the direction of Romania as a good place to start if more ancient places were out of the question. So, I delved deeper into the origins.

O
r
i
g
i
n
s

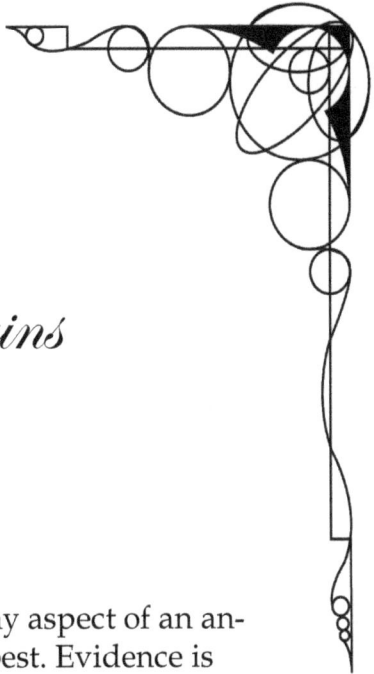

2 - Origins

Researching any aspect of an ancient civilization is subjective at best. Evidence is often fragmented and contaminated by the erosive nature of time. So, we build what resembles a fitting image of a particular culture using the pieces of the puzzle we have and then allow our minds to fill in the gaps. Paleography, too, is often cryptic, and even within its own time, writing was often only known by the priestly and royal classes. Any break in its physical transmission through time caused disruptions and inaccuracies. Mythology and the origins of certain superstitions are even more elusive since such lores and yarns were often orally transmitted, undergoing edits and modifications, hence filtered through the imagination of the orator. I jotted notes during my research as to what made sense to me in an attempt to reconcile superstition with scientific fact, if indeed any evidence was found to substantiate such.

Our knowledge of classical vampirism comes

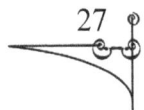

down to us through an accumulation of folklore, beliefs, myths, and history. Inspired by visual minds, fired by natural wonders, and blended by the transitory crossroads of many different cultures, they have thus reached us, finessed by the crafty fingers of rhetoric through the words of silver-tongued storytellers.

In ancient rituals, blood representing life was shed through human sacrifice to appease the gods. Such rituals were almost universal and for logical reasons. From a religious standpoint, the worship of pagan gods or nature may have begun in Mesopotamia, the cradle of civilization, especially the region which later became ancient Babylonia, a union of two earlier neighboring kingdoms, that of Sumer and Akkad. As man then eventually spread out across the globe, he would have brought elements of primitive worship with him, which is why common threads of belief and ritual are found in vastly different cultures throughout the world. In Genesis chapter 9, Noah is told by God the significance of blood to him, that blood signified the life of a person, which was sacred and not to be eaten but respectfully returned to the ground. In time, myths and the belief of the dead craving blood for life arose, leading to the invention of such creatures as the Lilu in Babylonian mythology.

Lilith, a Babylonian creature, comes to us through the proto-Semitic root for "night" and is translated as "female night being." She was believed to harm male children. Cuneiform inscriptions cause some to argue that she was a storm demon, the Sumerian "Lil" meaning wind or air. Descriptions found in the mythical story of Gilgamesh paint Lilith as a

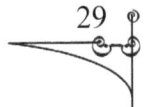

Lilith 1892

female demon. She is often associated with the depiction found in the Burney Relief circa the 18th century BCE, which shows a nude female having both the wings and talons of a bird of prey flanked on either side by owls. It was only centuries later in Babylonian mythology that the characteristics of the Lilu morphed and eventually took the shape of vampire-esque spirits, female spirits that roamed the dark hours, killing babies and pregnant women.

The Talmud also makes reference to Lilith, which would eventually lead to the Jewish mystical belief of Lilith as a night demon and a wife of Adam other than Eve. According to Biblical scholars, this is based upon the erroneous and overly liberal interpretation of two separate verses found in the book of Genesis. Man and woman are first created; then later in Genesis, more details are given. Eve is created from the rib of Adam, leading these mystics to conclude that these two separate occurrences refer to two different women. However, the Holy Scriptures do not mention a second woman in name or form. Mainstream Abrahamic religions and Biblical scholars are of the same opinion that Eve is the only woman spoken of in Genesis. This mystic belief in Lilith, however, was said to be nonexistent or at least extremely vague before the Middle Ages and tied more to Jewish mysticism than mainstream Judaism. A reference found in the Dead Sea Scrolls, "Song for a Sage," shows from earlier times an awareness of Lilith and her association with supernatural creatures, thus alluding to the probable formation of what she would later become by Jewish definition in the Middle Ages.

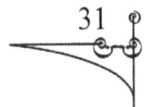

However, the Essenes responsible for the Dead Sea Scrolls, again, were not considered a part of mainstream Judaism but a fringe sect of it. Another unscriptural belief employed an amulet with the names of three angels inscribed on it, which was placed around the neck of newborn boys to ward off the Lilin until their circumcision.

The Jewish nation would have had exposure to Babylonian mythology during their bondage there in the 6th century BCE, and so Lilith's growth in Jewish mysticism isn't that surprising despite efforts to keep their worship clean and uncontaminated; traditions and language are always affected by other cultures they contact. In Isaiah chapter 34, the King James Version uses the term "screech owl," or Lilit, in standard Hebrew. It is the only mention of the word in the Bible. Such early versions, however, often took liberties for the sake of prose. Also, without access to the large amount of original language texts we have today, the literal essence of words was often lost when translated. Better choices could have and should have been used. A better understanding of the original languages, less reliance on church dogma, and a greater body of other reference material to work from might also have helped. Other sources point to even earlier times, such as the bloodsucking Akhkharu from Sumerian mythology.

The screech owl is also the primary source of the Roman Strix, a nocturnal bird of ill omen that fed on the blood and flesh of humans. Greek mythology tells us of Agrios and Oreios, both of whom were transformed into wild animals as punishment for

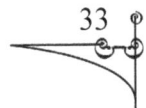

Lamia 1909

cannibalism. Polyphonte, their mother, became the Strix. Greek culture was eventually absorbed by the rise of the Roman empire, and thus, Greek mythology became Roman mythology with only minor changes to names and places. Pliny, writing in the first century, confessed little knowledge of these night creatures, though they were to play an important later role in the formation of the Romanian Vampire.

Another creature of interest in Greek mythology is Lamia, the daughter of Poseidon and Lybie, who was the personification of Libya and queen of Libya herself. Zeus himself loved her, and Hera's jealousy turned her into a monster. Hera killed all of her children except Scylla. Lamia was unable to close her eyes, a curse that placed an image of her dead children always before her. Her envy then turned towards childbearing mortals, which she satisfied by devouring their newborn children. She had the body of a serpent and the torso, breasts, and head of a woman. Blood-drinking female vampire-like spirits came to be called Lamiai, which in later medieval lore became the succubi (singular: succubus). These were female night demons who targeted men, especially monks, while they were sleeping, having intercourse to defile them and drain them of energy, sometimes to the point of death.

The far-off land of India also had its own blood-drinking creatures, such as BrahmarakShasa and Kali, who were also endowed with fangs. Their belief in reincarnation alludes to another probable source of vampires being thought of as undead. Kali, also female, and the goddess Durga battled the de-

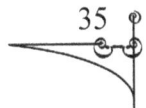

Bram Stoker

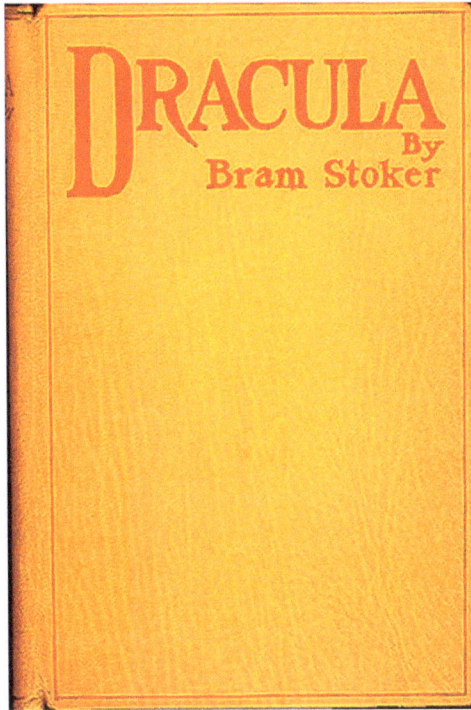

First edition print

1897

mon Raktabija, who could reproduce himself from drops of blood, ultimately winning the battle by drinking all his blood. Kali becomes Sara, or the Black goddess of the Gypsies. Gypsies, being nomadic, eventually found their way into Europe. They continue to have a strong presence in many countries throughout Europe even to this day, including Romania. The fact of the matter is that their beliefs and folklore also followed to become blended with local lore.

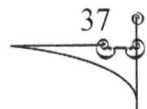

J Sheridan LeFanu

Western concepts of vampirism come primarily to us through works of fiction such as *Dracula* (1897) by Irish writer Bram Stoker, which is also based upon other vampiric tales such as *Carmilla* (1872) by Sheridan LeFanu. It is said *Carmilla* may, in turn, have been influenced by "The Vampyre" (1819) by John William Polidori, which was a work originally attributed to Lord Byron. However, "Christabel" (1797–1800), a lengthy unfinished poem by Samuel Taylor Coleridge, has a closer resemblance to *Carmilla* due to its atmospheric ambiance and the fact that the story revolves around the sensual relationship between two women. Western tales of vampirism all owe their essence to Romanian folklore, with possible elements of Celtic mythology in Stoker's work. Also, Stoker's experience with death and the systematic forced starvation at the hands of the British, played against the backdrop of Christianity, may have played a role in his composition.

In Romanian mythology, they are called *Strigoi*, and the term *Moroi* is also used to describe these undead that arise from the grave at night to prey upon the living and have the power to transform into animals and shapeshift. Their condition is attributed to a curse from a long list of anomalies such as premature birth, extra hair, an extra nipple, a caul, a tail, and being born out of wedlock or in the presence of a black cat, to name but a few of numerous superstitions. They are said to have fair to ginger hair, blue eyes, and a double heart. In Slovenian mythology, "Striga" are usually female and can only be killed while they are feasting on the living.

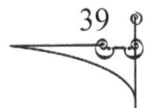

Vampire stories might also have been influenced by a rare illness called porphyria. The disease disrupts the production of heme. People with extreme cases of this hereditary disease can be so sensitive to sunlight that they can even sunburn through heavy cloud cover, causing them to be nocturnal and avoid all light. People with porphyria can also have red eyes and teeth, resulting from a buildup of red heme intermediates (porphyrins). Certain forms of porphyria are also associated with neurological symptoms, which can create psychiatric disorders. However, the hypotheses that porphyria sufferers crave the heme in human blood or that the consumption of blood might ease the symptoms of porphyria are based on ignorance.

Despite the heavy influence of cross-cultural mythology in defining vampirism, there are also some actual historical elements that have become homogenized into vampire lore, especially Vlad Tepes III.

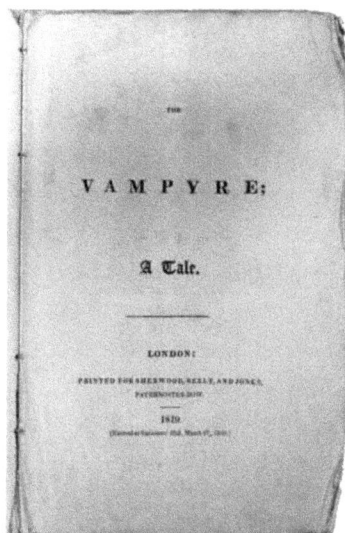

VAMPYRE;

A Tale.

LONDON:

PRINTED FOR SHERWOOD, NEELY, AND JONES,
PATERNOSTER-ROW.

1819.

1819 Manuscript

Christabel (excerpt) c 1797 - 1800

There she sees a damsel bright,
Dressed in a silken robe of white,
That shadowy in the moonlight shone :
The neck that made that white robe wan,
Her stately neck, and arms were bare ;
Her blue-veined feet unsandal'd were ;
And wildly glittered here and there
The gems entangled in her hair.
I guess, 'twas frightful there to see
A lady so richly clad as she--
Beautiful exceedingly !

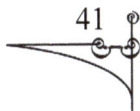

41

Again the wild-flower wine she drank :
Her fair large eyes 'gan glitter bright,
And from the floor whereon she sank,
　　The lofty lady stood upright :
　　She was most beautiful to see,
　　Like a lady of a far countrée.

Her silken robe, and inner vest,
Dropt to her feet, and full in view,
Behold ! her bosom, and half her side—
A sight to dream of, not to tell !
O shield her ! shield sweet Christabel !

And lay down by the Maiden's side !—
And in her arms the maid she took,

And with low voice and doleful look
These words did say :
'In the touch of this bosom there worketh a spell,
Which is lord of thy utterance, Christabel !
Thou knowest to-night, and wilt know to-morrow
This mark of my shame, this seal of my sorrow ;

And Christabel awoke and spied
The same who lay down by her side—

So deeply had she drunken in
That look, those shrunken serpent eyes,
That all her features were resigned

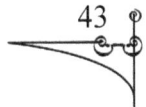

Carmilla (excerpt) 1872

She caressed me with her hands, and lay down beside me on the bed, and drew me towards her, smiling; I felt immediately delightfully soothed, and fell asleep again. I was wakened by a sensation as if two needles ran into my breast very deep at the same moment, and I cried loudly. The lady started back, with her eyes fixed on me, and then slipped down upon the floor, and, as I thought, hid herself under the bed. ....

Her looks lost nothing in daylight-she was certainly the most beautiful creature I had ever seen, and the unpleas-ant remembrance of the face presented in my early dream, had lost the effect of the first unexpected recognition.

She was above the middle height of women. I shall begin by describing her. She was slender, and wonderfully graceful. Except that her movements were languid-very languid- indeed, there was nothing in her appearance to indicate an invalid. Her complexion was rich and brilliant; her features were small and beautifully formed; her eyes large, dark, and lustrous; her hair was quite wonderful, I never saw hair so magnificently thick and long when it was down about her shoulders; I have often placed my hands under it, and laughed with wonder at its weight. It was exquisitely fine and soft, and in colour a rich very dark brown, with something of gold. I loved to let it down, tumbling with its own weight, as, in her room, she lay back in her chair talking in her sweet low voice, I used to fold and braid it, and spread it out and play with it. Heavens! If I had but known all!

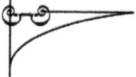

It was all summed up in three very vague disclosures:
First~Her name was Carmilla.
Second~Her family was very ancient and noble.
Third~Her home lay in the direction of the west.

Sometimes after an hour of apathy, my strange and beautiful companion would take my hand and hold it with a fond pressure, renewed again and again; blushing softly, gazing in my face with languid and burning eyes, and breathing so fast that her dress rose and fell with the tumultuous respiration. It was like the ardour of a lover; it embarrassed me; it was hateful and yet over-powering; and with gloating eyes she drew me to her, and her hot lips travelled along my cheek in kisses; and she would whisper, almost in sobs, "You are mine, you shall be mine, you and I are one for ever." Then she has thrown her-self back in her chair, with her small hands over her eyes, leaving me trembling.
She kissed me silently.

"I am sure, Carmilla, you have been in love; that there is, at this moment, an affair of the heart going on."
"I have been in love with no one, and never shall," she whispered, "unless it should be with you."

How beautiful she looked in the moonlight!
Shy and strange was the look with which she quickly hid her face in my neck and hair, with tumultuous sighs, that seemed almost to sob, and pressed in mine a hand that trembled.

Her soft cheek was glowing against mine. "Darling, dar-ling," she murmured, "I live in you; and you would die for me, I love you so."
I started from her.

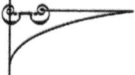

She was gazing on me with eyes from which all fire, all meaning had flown, and a face colourless and apathetic.

"Is there a chill in the air, dear?" she said drowsily. "I almost shiver; have I been dreaming? Let us come in. Come; come; come in."

"You look ill, Carmilla; a little faint. You certainly must take some wine," I said.

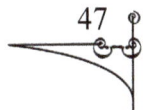

47

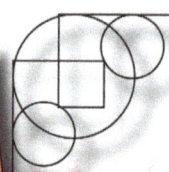

Vlad Tepes

Dracul

Birth

Death

3 - Vlad Tepes the Impaler

Bram Stoker doesn't specifically mention the person of Vlad Tepes in his magnum opus. However, the title of his work and its setting of Transylvania create an obvious trail of breadcrumbs leading us back from the pages of fiction to the fertile soils of fact. One character emerges as the best source for Stoker's inspiration: the historical figure Vlad Tepes III. Vlad the Impaler, as he is commonly known, was the son of Vlad II Dracul. ("Drac" in Romanian means devil, and the "ul" adds the definite article to it, hence becoming Dracul or "the devil;" however, Vlad Tepes was also a member of the Order of the Dragon, a knight's order dedicated to fighting the Turks and with whom his father was associated, hence the title of Dracula, which could also mean son of the Dragon in reference to the order itself (the roots for both dragon and devil being similar)).

Vlad (Tepes) Dracula lived from circa 1431 to 1476 and ruled the region of Wallachia, not Transyl-

vania, as commonly believed, though he was born in Sighisoara, a prominent city of Transylvania. Wallachia was a Province of Romania bordered by Transylvania and Moldavia in the north and east, Bulgaria and the Black Sea to the south, and Hungry to the northwest. Sovereign rule, though heredity, was maintained through an election made by the aristocracy, wealthy and influential classes who chose from the Royal household their ruler, not through a system of primogeniture, in which rule would have passed to the eldest son. As with such systems of that time, paranoia also accompanied such power. Politics was rife with deception and scheming, which often turned bloody in order to exterminate any rivalry or competition for the throne, even within bloodlines. With Islam and the Ottoman Empire practically on their doorstep, eastern Christianity struggled to maintain its defenses.

Hungary was also reaching its peak in power under John Hunyadi, the White Knight of Hungary, and his son King Corvinus. The prince of Wallachia could really only exist as a vassal to the dominant Hungarian power. In 1448 Dracula managed to briefly seize the Wallachian throne with Turkish support. Within two months, though, Hunyadi forced Dracula to surrender the throne and flee into exile to his cousin, the Prince of Moldavia. He eventually returned and killed the Danesti prince whom Hunyadi had originally replaced him with — with the backing of Hunyadi himself because the Danesti prince had become pro-Turkish, angering the Hungarian ruler.

The great city of Constantinople, a Christian

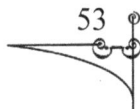

This woodcut from that period shows
Vlad the Impaler dining after he had
thousands of merchants and officials
of the Transylvanian city of Brasov
impaled for defying his authority. He is
seen here feasting amongst a forest of
stakes clad with their grisly victims, some
of which are still alive while others are
dead. Before the table, an executioner
dismembers other victims.

stronghold for over a thousand years, which had shielded Europe and Christendom from Islam, fell to the Ottomans in 1453. Hunyadi was forced to retaliate, thus planning and launching attacks in 1456, while Dracula, at the same time, launched his attack at Wallachia. The throne of Wallachia was once again in Dracula's possession in 1456, though Hunyadi's army was defeated, and he was slain in the battle of Belgrade.

Vlad Dracula's main ruling period stretched from 1456 to 1462. He was said to be a skilled soldier and horseman, and in one particular battle at the beginning of his reign, he was said to have beheaded the leader of attacking forces in arm-to-arm combat. His capital city was Tirgoviste, though his castle was located some distance away, fortified by the mountain slopes and by the Arges River. Most of the atrocities associated with Dracula's name took place in these years. It was during this reign that he committed gruesome acts not only upon the Turks but also on his own people. Turkish forces eventually forced him to flee to Transylvania and seek help from King Corvinus, who had assumed his father's power. Rather than being welcomed, he was imprisoned in a tower near Buda for twelve years.

In 1447 Vlad's father had been killed by local nobles wielding the power of warlords. His older brother was also killed; he was said to have been tortured, blinded, and eventually burned alive. Death by impalement wasn't unique to Vlad; it existed down through the ages and was also employed by the Ottoman Empire. Perhaps all of this played into Vlad

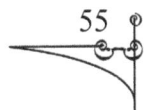

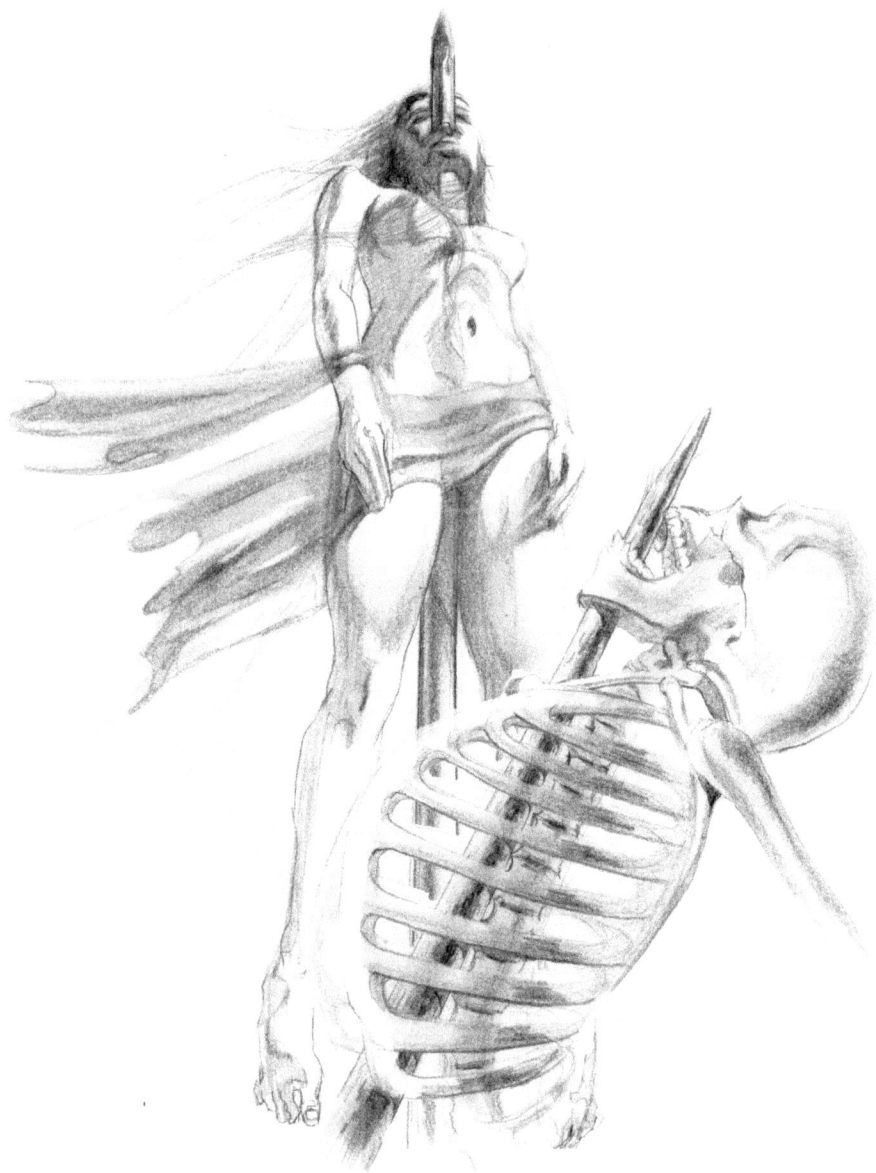

becoming the monster he did.

His first wife was said to have committed suicide by throwing herself from the castle heights into the river Arges rather than allowing herself to be captured by the Turks. Radu, his brother, who was merely a figurehead under the Ottoman Sultan, assumed power over Wallachia. Upon release he was given forces to fight and regain the throne in 1476. Dracula did renounce his Eastern Orthodox faith while in captivity, but rather than turning to the powers of darkness, he embraced Catholicism, which wasn't really that much different.

It was Vlad's inhumane cruelty that struck fear into his opponents. Oiled stakes sharpened to blunt points to ensure a slow death were forced into his victims, generally entering through the anus or vagina. Others were sharpened to puncture flesh and often exited the mouth, shoulders, or torso. This was done with the use of horses tied to each leg so that the victim was pulled and forcibly skewered. Victims were also impaled through other orifices. Even infants were impaled with their mothers on the same stakes. It often took days for victims to die, and the decomposing corpses throughout the land were left impaled for months, causing the stench and visions of death to abound throughout the land. Reports indicate that an army once turned away at the banks of the river Danube upon being greeted by twenty thousand rotting corpses impaled near the river.

Death by impalement wasn't the only torture. Dracula used a plethora of tools and torture methods

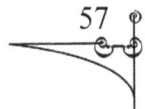

Vlad the Impaler and the Turkish Envoy

1880

that would make Satan squirm, such as nails hammered into the head, skinning, mutilation of sexual organs, especially in women, boiling oil, scalping, dismemberment, and disembowelment, to name but a few. Many of his victims were his own people, with no exceptions made as to age, sex, class, or social status. It is reported that Vlad once wrote to a warring ally stating, "I have killed peasants, men and women, young and old...We killed 23,884 Turks, without counting those whom we burned in homes or the Turks whose heads were cut off by our soldiers..." All in total, Vlad may have killed up to 80,000 people by various means.

In 1476, with only a small army at his disposal and abandoned by his people for his prior atrocities, he met his fate against an overwhelming Turkish army. He was killed in battle in Bucharest in December of that year, beheaded, and his head impaled on a stake in Constantinople. He is said to have been buried at Snagov monastery outside of Bucharest. His grave, when exhumed centuries later, showed a mysteriously empty crypt, adding fuel to the myth.

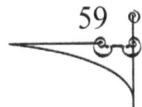

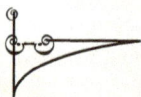

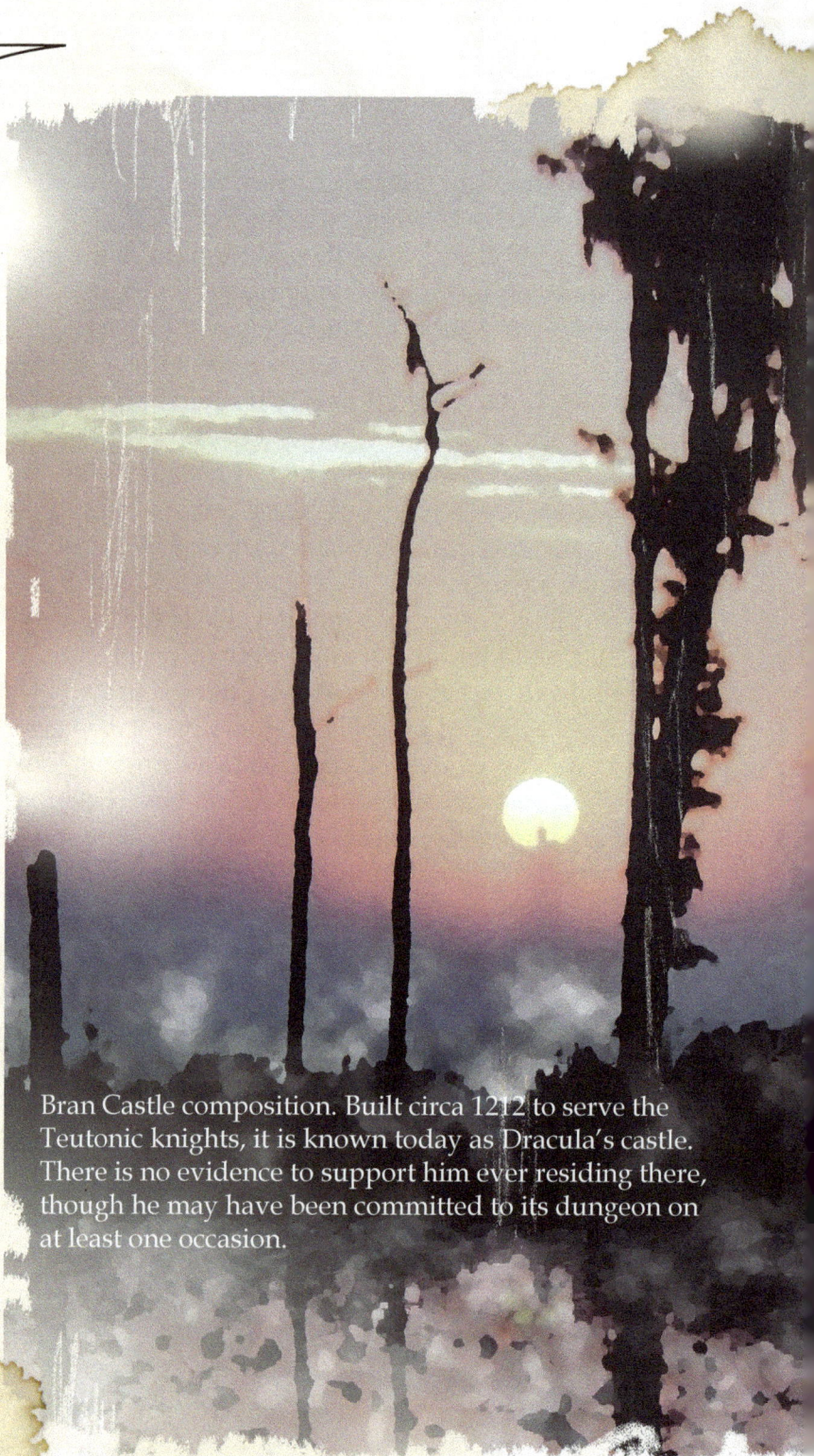

Bran Castle composition. Built circa 1212 to serve the
Teutonic knights, it is known today as Dracula's castle.
There is no evidence to support him ever residing there,
though he may have been committed to its dungeon on
at least one occasion.

4 - The Land Beyond the Forest

Every time I sat back in the evening with a glass of wine and contemplated the idea, my rational mind interjected, and it was during one such period when I wrote back to Mr. Stefanistsa stating my reasons for declining his offer. No sooner than he could have possibly received the letter, I was invited to a manor in County Meath, a few hours northwest of Dublin. I was fetched from my home and escorted by carriage to the grounds of a large estate where I expected to meet the gentleman who had prodded my curiosity.

Though this was the house he resided in during visits to Ireland, he was not there, and I learned that the house stood vacant for eleven months of the year yet employed a large staff year-round. I was quietly escorted to the library, a magnificent room that made me envious. It alone was larger than my house and my neighbor's house combined in width and depth but far taller still. It stood three levels high, accessible by spiral staircases at both ends of the room and balconies hugging the bookshelves, which could be accessed by attached rolling ladders.

I refused tea when offered (it upset my stomach) but opted for coffee as an alternative choice when asked, which was a beverage seldom found in Irish homes. While I was sitting and sipping on the rich, earthy flavors of my Arabica and admiring the surroundings, a man of few words entered and uncovered a glass cabinet. Before me stood a long rectangular case, visible through all sides and with its top removed. "Dr. Lucard, please feel free to examine," he said in a monotone and then left without further word.

Within the case was what looked like a partial human skeleton. As I approached, I saw a partially reassembled rib cage, a humerus, and other bone fragments. Beneath was a canvas with the outline of a body drawn to measurements calculated from the partial remains. Sex could not be determined, but human it certainly looked. When I turned, the man dismissed himself silently, leaving me with an envelope in hand which stated the obvious that was in my mind. Mr. Stefanistsa, in his letter, prompted me to turn the skeleton's posterior aspect upwards to see if anything sparked my interest.

I gently rolled the broken rib cage, which had been reassembled with wire, and before it was even turned, I immediately noticed an anatomical anomaly. For one, the scapula was an unusual shape, more elongated and narrower than the triangular shape found in humans, and it seemed to sit better towards a more medial part of the back. I hadn't

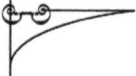

noticed it from the anterior view, as the canvas didn't offer much contrast. Rolled over, I also noticed a crater in the scapula, too perfectly formed to be a defect. It looked like another ball and socket joint, though not the one for the humerus—it was too shifted and dorsal for that, which would have placed the arm to the back. My mind began reasoning and fabricating possibilities: a mutation or deformation, perhaps. Maybe it was something else, not human, but what animal has an anatomical torso close to that of a human other than primates? As I imagined candidates, it still didn't make sense. The hollow in the scapula was still unique. If this was to support another large bone like the humerus, what was it used for? Wings did come to mind, but even birds don't have this anatomical makeup. A sternum and clavicle, or possibly a furcula, which is a forked bone formed by the fusion of the two clavicles found in birds to aid flight, would have shed more light on the partial remains, but these, too, were missing.

    I was now starting to believe that Mr. Stefanistsa was more rational than I had given him credit for. I wanted to return with some other specialized scientists from the university to implore their opinion, but my request was denied, and I was sworn to secrecy. I did, however, sketch what I saw, and when I presented it before colleagues, the best answer I received was perhaps an extinct prehistoric flyer like a pterodactyl. However, what I had seen were skeletal remains, not fossils; these were the remains of something far more recent—within the last hundred years or so, depending on preservation.

By now, summer was approaching, and with the time I would have away from work, my norm was to read and write. This year was to be no different if that stranger had not crossed my path. Visions of far-off places excited my mind. Occasionally, at night, I would see Mrs. Kelly's sad face. I knew she believed her husband was long gone, but had he been back in Ireland, it would have made no difference due to his sick nature. I think what she sought, though, was closure.

Europe was in a peaceful lull; industrialism and science were the new religions in a world that appeared to be spinning faster. Ireland was still having its own private quarrel with Britain, which was normal in the daily affairs of Irish life. Politics was something else I never got caught up in, though I did believe in a free Ireland. I also believed in a free world, and I sympathized most with the bystanders affected by conflict, those not involved in arm-to-arm combat. I found it hard to place my faith in a society that promoted itself as civilized while the blood of one another still coated our hands — it was a simple dichotomy. Fighting for freedom or peace was like making love for virginity or writing for illiteracy. Nevertheless, there was a tension, an uneasiness in the Irish air.

The alluring tranquility in Europe stretched out its hand in invitation. A summer in Romania seemed now all the more appealing: a summer with sun perhaps, something Ireland seldom received except on the occasional unexpected day between rain and storm. Such an opportunity might never appear

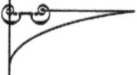

again, and who could say, if I served my benefactor well, he might fund other research projects of my choosing.

My latest response to Mr. Stefanistsa had been a maybe. On May 12th, before even agreeing to the assignment, details concerning my itinerary, fares, and accommodations were already arranged and arrived by mail. There were no excuses for me not to go. I packed lightly: two changes of clothes besides those I was wearing, a few books, a journal, pen, and pencil, and last and most importantly, some tools of the trade: scalpel, forceps, saw, hammer, etc., and a small portable microscope. On the morning of June 10th, I boarded a ship to France via England, and from France, I traveled directly by rail to Bucharest, making carriage connections along the way, when necessary, as the train route broke in areas. A sleeper car offered me the rest I required on this six-day journey. I dined with the gentry, a little out of my league but paid for nonetheless; however, I never felt inadequate or embarrassed. My education more than compensated for my underclass demeanor, which the gentry generally always gave a concession to.

One evening, while sipping a glass of wine, I lost focus on an article I was reading. The cloak of night had fallen. We had left Belgrade that morning, and as I attempted to see detail in the blackness outside, my dark reflection in the windowpane and the repetitive sound and movement of the train had a hypnotic effect, causing my mind to meander, eventually stopping upon something I had not previously given thought to. Every myth is born out

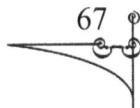

of some factual basis, whether great or fragmented. Vampires appear to have a history in which even the history of that time itself is too old to reconcile and substantiate with any degree of certainty, and so we are left to base our belief on faith or dismiss these threads until pivotal hard evidence is uncovered.

I wondered, as far as Western knowledge of vampires was concerned, whether those who wrote about it were privy to some gnosis of something beyond the place of common knowledge. I found it ironic that Byron, who had a malformed foot making him partially lame and was one of the earliest Westerners to mention these creatures, died relatively young of a strange fever exasperated by bloodletting while fighting for Greek independence from the Ottoman Empire, the same Empire Vlad Tepes had fought against centuries earlier. And then Polidori, who had used Byron's material as the basis for his story, was plagued by depression and died mysteriously at an even younger age, during Byron's own life. Le Fanu fell into a deep depression when his wife died and was said to have penned his stories from midnight till dawn with two candle sticks by each side; one wonders how he had the energy to hold a full-time day job and care for four children with his wife gone. Le Fanu himself reportedly said that he was striving for "the equilibrium between natural and the super-natural, the super-natural phenomena being explained by natural theories — and people left to choose whichever hypothesis pleased them most." Stoker had a debilitating illness when he was younger, which, in union with his belief system, inspired his story. Was there a peculiar thread tying all these men together, or was this just my hyper-imagination at work? I guess every individual has peculiarities in life — it's part of what makes us individuals.

Romania was also moving forwards along with the rest of Europe with the explosion of industrialism and social development. It, too, was also the land of some of Europe's great doctors, such as Victor Babes and Gheorghe Marinescu. I wondered why such great men of the time had not been heralded by the powers that selected me, hardly even known within my own city. Ironic again was the fact that Dr. Babes was known for his work with blood-borne pathogens, some of which were fatal to man, while one of Marinescu's eponyms was "Marinescu's hand," a cold, blue oedematous hand with lividity of the skin seen from neurological lesions. Such areas of study and observation were also key areas concerning vampirism, and so I pondered on the fact that they may have also been privy somehow to the gnosis I was yet to acquire. Or was this some elaborate conspiracy unfolding upon the chessboard of time on which I was a pawn?

Bucharest, on arrival, seemed just like Dublin but with a different odor. Perhaps it was just the drizzle that added a drab grey filter to a city already painted grey with aged granite. Children begging littered the streets just like in Dublin, though the weather was somewhat warmer. After some time en route to my hotel, I did begin to notice differences. Some of the architecture displayed an Eastern design

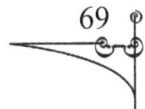

not seen in Ireland. Very few cultures had shaped Ireland's history with its remoteness and the seeming nothingness beyond its west coast but the violent Atlantic. Romania, though, was a cultural crossroad, the stomping ground between east and west, and thus more volatile to outside influence. My hotel was as expected: a regular hotel, not too fancy, not too shabby, just right for my means, though I ate at a restaurant farther down the street in a fancier hotel, which would have been beyond my means back home, but here it was just right, serving food I was accustomed to, as my palate is a fussy one. I took a few days to settle in, walk the streets, and take in the sights before moving on again to my final destination.

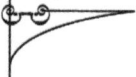

5 - A Summer of Strangers

*T*hree evenings later, while dining at the Bucuresti Grand restaurant on Maghera, I was reading as I generally did while dining alone when a draft of cool air with hints of jasmine lifted my face from the pages below, only to catch the glance of a lady making her way into the hotel. I should say, rather, that it was her glance that caught me, which was followed by a simple smile of acknowledgment to the manager greeting her before she disappeared behind the marble Romanesque colonnades and tall tropical plants which lined the hallway. I looked up occasionally in that direction to see if I'd see her again—her stare, those large dark eyes were captivating and still before me for the remainder of the evening. Leaving the hotel that evening, I was approached by the desk clerk, who handed me a small white card on a tray. It was a business card with an embossed crest on it, the name Ruxandra above it, and an address beneath it, all in elegant,

raised typography. The card had a note on the back, handwritten as elegantly as the print on the front. All it said was, "Please visit when you reach Bucegi." The card, too, had the scent of jasmine mingled with another aromatic nocturnal blossom I did not recognize — it was the woman I had seen earlier. I wondered how she even knew of me or my itinerary, for that matter. The hotel clerk was of no help at all.

Prahova Valley was the area surrounding Bucegi, where Dr. Kelly had penned his last words. The valley was the main passageway between the old principalities of Wallachia and Transylvania. Interestingly, the Bucegi mountains were said to have included the Thracian holy mountain of Kogainon, which was home to Zalmoxis, considered a god to some and a man to others. He was said to have traveled to ancient Egypt and was said to have received mystic knowledge concerning immortality. The elevations here are not high by mountain standards. Omu Peak only stood approximately 8100 feet above sea level, though its steep slopes had some unique rock features and treacherous escarpments. Like the rest of my trip to this point, everything had been arranged with clockwork precision.

On leaving Bucharest on the fourth day, I was fetched by carriage. Bucegi was approximately one hundred miles due north; however, I had not planned on heading directly there. Other places of interest, such as Tirgoviste, were to be visited, causing a slight diversion. I was greeted by a grey morning when I awoke, but the sun peeked out from behind a cotton cloud as we left Bucharest, and before long,

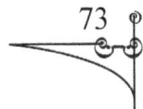

the greyness of the cityscape turned to the greenness of rural nature warmed by buttered rays from a now brilliant sun. Romania, at this point, didn't resemble Ireland in any way. I could feel the sun's heat on my body even at such an early time of the morning. Trees speckled the countryside in abundance. Ireland's greenery was gently rolling hills of grasslands, bald in areas to the rock, devoid of trees, scraped bare by the wickedness of men and a harsh, relentless climate.

I spent a few days in Tirgoviste and was fortunate enough to meet a young lad, perhaps fifteen or so, who had noticed me struggling to communicate with a merchant. He introduced himself as Petr. Petr's father had been a civil servant and had spent a number of years working in Britain as a translator for the government, and as a result, he spoke English very well, maybe better than I did. Upon meeting with his parents, I had a request which was gratefully honored: for the price of a week's wage paid to his parents, he was released into my care to accompany me in my travels for a month or so, as I would certainly need a translator. Petr himself I would pay the price of a few bob or leu here and there throughout the trip.

Vampire folklore was woven into the psyche of the Romanian people, or at least those living in rural areas, where superstitions always appeared stronger. Although most could recount such tales, to go beyond these tales lacked anything of substance I could follow save the exploits of Vlad Tepes III, a history I was already acquainted with. The mountains were said to have fearsome beasts that preyed upon men,

but that was a generalized, unfounded assumption that could be attributed to a host of wild animals such as wolves or bears.

We entered a wilderness that appeared untouched by humans. The Carpathian mountains seemed to rise like a fortress wall encircling Romania, the slopes of which were forested. Dusk was falling when we reached Bucegi; my bones were sore from the unpaved, bumpy roads. Bucegi came upon us quickly and appeared as a small town with no hotels. I didn't fancy staying at an inn because of Petr and to avoid a spectacle since we were foreigners noticeable to the locals who seldom saw anyone through these parts, so we found lodging in a guest house, which was really just a private residence with a spare room holding two beds and a tall, narrow chest of drawers. I was glad to see a bed on which to rest.

We were known before long, new faces amongst regulars. The owner of the inn remembered Dr. Kelly, which didn't surprise me, as Dr. Kelly was fond of his drink. The innkeeper smiled as he recalled that Mr. Kelly would have become one of them if his accident hadn't happened. His generous ways were shown in the habit of buying drinks for the locals, even the entire pub on more than one occasion, which was an act of kindness seldom seen, not due to any lack of kindness itself on behalf of the people here but due to the fact that people didn't have such means. I was shown the general direction Dr. Kelly had headed in on his last day seen. "Into the terrible forest, he went and never came out," was what we were told. Every day over the course of a week or so,

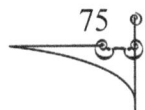

he had gone into the forest in the same direction, as if something in there had caught his attention, which kept him returning to the same place.

The forest before us began abruptly with a clearing down the center, a shallow vale flanked by coniferous trees on either side spanning approximately fifty feet. The vale rose slightly over the course of a mile or so straight ahead of us before abruptly rising with a steep gradient, closing in with a populated forest. The forest then tapered into a triangular finish like an arrow pointing beyond to an ominous monument of sheer rock. Another valley appeared above the tree line, cloaked in shadow, walled on either side by vertical granite rock faces, both of which culminated in two peaks. The one on the left was very pointed, while the one on the right was flatter but peaked on both sides. All this lay straight ahead of us. The forest was dense from the beginning, so we picked the clearing to travel by since it was as good a place as any. We would begin in the morning at first light. I spent that day going short distances into the forest on either side of the vale to see if it yielded anything hidden from our initial vantage point.

The following morning I decided to leave Petr behind, as I didn't want to be responsible for anything happening to him, but he insisted it was all a big adventure to him, though I had held back when telling him the purpose of my trip. Our destination was straight ahead towards the mountains, for lack of a better plan. There was a lot of ground to cover, and we were without a single clue to go on. The town didn't keep very complete or accurate records. It seemed that people died as people do within any demographics, and no cause for alarm arose. I was still vague on why I was even here — to continue Dr. Kelly's research, but without any supporting material. Sure, memories of him were here, but nothing physical, nothing tangible. His belongings and equipment probably disappeared shortly after he did. People did go missing here, but even when a person left this area in broad daylight, never to return, the locals spun yarns fabricating a superstitious version of the story. Much of that day we spent hiking, just Petr and me. I didn't expect to find anything, and I didn't, but if for nothing else, the exercise was welcomed. I did, however, get to gauge distances a bit better. Every day for a few weeks, we hiked the surrounding areas of the mountain, getting a sense of the lay of the land.

The townsfolk didn't seem too concerned about the mountain, though they said it was haunted, and vampires did exist in the mind of almost every Wallachian. There was always a story to be told. Even the local priest informed me of a girl who had died some years ago in a neighboring town. Noises had been heard from her coffin while she was being buried, and those associated with the burial were plagued, so her body was exhumed a week later, on a Sunday, for its holy significance. Her body was found in a contorted position with scratch marks upon the wood inside the coffin, not in the peaceful state she was initially put to rest in. The priest had then driven a stake through her chest, pinning her body to the

ground so the body could not raise itself, shoved a flat stone in her mouth, and then blessed it. These were the kinds of clippings I had read about, reported in papers throughout Europe, even within the past fifty years or so. My conclusion was, as most doctors would conclude, catalepsy, in which a person exhibits the symptoms of death but is still alive in a frozen-like state (muscular rigidity being a symptom along with a slowed metabolism). Waking later to find themselves confined, they eventually suffocate while attempting to free themselves. The human mind is a powerful thing: when there are gaps in our knowledge, we have the tendency to fill those gaps with a fabricated logic. To some it is done by means of superstition; to others, like myself, it is simply ignorance, and there is a rational filler for the gap we just haven't found yet.

Reminiscing one evening on the back porch, I had a feeling of guilt. On an all-expense paid trip, I had been here a month with nothing to show for it. I was about to write Mr. Stefanistsa the same letter I had written two weeks ago. In ways I felt silly, a man of science on a witch hunt. What would this do to my reputation within the scientific community? Perhaps the air of secrecy surrounding the entire event would help me play it down. I could tout it as the bohemian side of me seeking the experiences of exotic, far-off places. The dim light from the house illuminated the outside night for about twenty feet before losing its power to the darkness. Now and then black specks would erratically appear and disappear on its fringes, bats no doubt — if I listened intently, I could hear the flutter of their wings, only by sheer number,

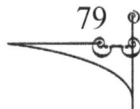

though. It made me recall one of the great spectacles I had seen when visiting Sydney, Australia. During the summer months, at dusk, a multitude of black silhouettes would take to the skies, fruit bats flying south towards the fruit groves to gorge themselves on ripening fruit. Our beautiful world of wonder — this break was doing me good. My glass now empty, the still quietness of the night embraced me with blanket warmth as I nodded off, drifting far away to dreamscapes.

There was a pass above the tree line we had found, a corridor that increased upwards, eventually bending out of sight. On either side stood vertical walls of rock that appeared to scale a thousand feet or so into the sky. Huge boulders dotted the corridor, making us look like ants amongst pebbles rounded by time and weather, though the walls of rock looked sharp and ragged, as though the mountain had abruptly split in two. We had been here a few times, but the stark, daunting natural monument before us took some time to become acquainted with. I was looking for an easy route on the east-facing wall since it was gathering the early morning sun at the entrance. Sometimes cracks revealed themselves as ledges. These walls were not the only way to the summit. We could have gone around and hiked up from either side, which was something we had already done on more than one occasion. A chute with plenty of hold had me leave my backpack with Petr as I climbed vertically about twenty feet above. This passage took me onto a ledge about three feet wide that followed the upwards direction of the stony corridor below. The ledge, however, was deceiving, and after a few minutes of traversing it, the levelness of it began to roll and slope off, making it too dangerous to proceed without safety equipment. It was upon returning, coming back down the chute while searching blindly for footholds with my feet when my right foot landed in a sticky, slippery substance. When I had reached eye level with it, I used a piece of loose slate to scrape its broken surface. It was a tar-like substance in consistency with the color of molasses in oxidated browns. It was organic, and feces did come to mind straight away, but its odor was unlike the unpleasantness of other animal feces. I wondered if it was guano. Though probable, I had never encountered it before, so I was unsure. There was also a large amount of it, which caused me to look up, half expecting to see a roost of bats in one of the overhanging rocks, but there was nothing — just rock and a vast, abyssal sky.

It had been almost six weeks since I had left Dublin. The locals had embraced me, and I had even picked up some basic vocabulary in the local tongue. To date, nothing had been found, nor any trace of Dr. Kelly. I knew time, patience, and persistence were the touchstones to successful science, but I couldn't help feeling useless and inadequate. I still didn't have a clear picture of what I was looking for. Much of the material I had read I didn't believe; normally, one enters a scientific endeavor with an objective and conviction, but I had neither here. The only thing that had kept me here this long was my promise and what I considered a salaried working vacation. I returned

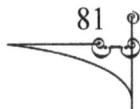

Petr home for a weekend, and I was able to extend his stay with me for another month after offering his family another week's wage.

The local town council was familiar with Dr. Kelly and his research. Mr. Stefanistsa was also known to them and had opened an account to pay the council members and other city workers for supplies, manpower, or any other aid required to assist Dr. Kelly, which was now extended to me. So, I inquired about any reports regarding local deaths within the last twenty years or so of those suspected of being vampires. The town council's secretary confirmed there had been two that he personally knew of but also a third one before his time, going back further, perhaps forty or fifty years ago. Dr. Kelly had already exhumed one of the corpses in the cemetery who had died some years prior to his arrival. The town council had required him to file a report of the exhumation with the town secretary and recorder. With a visit to the town archives, I was able to read through it.

The woman he examined was an elderly woman who lived in a small cabin in the woods just northwest of the town. Due to her reclusiveness and antisocial and irreligious disposition, she had been labeled a witch and then later a vampire. As a result, Dr. Kelly couldn't find any physical evidence to substantiate such a claim. Her death was mostly likely from a failed immune system response to an unhealed hip fracture due to osteoporosis. After returning the report to the archives, the secretary pointed us in the direction of the local parish church and, speaking in Romanian, which Petr translated for me, said, "Go talk to Father Bucali."

6 - Breaking Ground

The church was literally a stone's throw from the city office, and so we strolled across the street to it. The church doors were wide open as we walked in. A local craftsman was behind the door repairing an old metal handle on the right-hand side, which had become loose. The church appeared to be oversized for how small the town was. We stood at the entrance to look around and found Father Bucali towards the back, quietly chattering with two altar boys, directing them as they were replacing the votive candles on a rack along the left wall of the church. Upon reaching him, I introduced myself by means of Petr, but Father Bucali replied in a soft accent, "I speak English," and looking at Petr sternly said, "You should know this." I inquired about the vampire burials. He nodded his head emphatically, saying "Yes, yes," as he walked down the aisle to the entrance of the church with Petr and I following behind.

Stepping outside, he pointed south down the

town's main street and said, "If you follow the street, you'll see an old cemetery on the right as you leave town. Inside, facing west, at the far end of the cemetery in the far-left corner, there are two graves next to each other. They are by themselves with no other graves around them and have large stone crucifixes laid out on top of the graves stretching the full length and width. Those buried there were vampires, both female." I was taken by the surety of his comment, as if there was no doubt in his mind about their true nature. I asked permission to exhume the graves and examine the corpses. Father Bucali clutched the beads and cross that hung around his neck, raised his eyes to heaven, muttered a few words in Latin in an undertone, and then blessed himself with a sign of the cross. "Yes, yes," he said, "but I must also be present to prevent evil from rising." Then he also told me to seek permission from the town magistrate, Mr. Nicolae Enache. I inquired about the third vampire burial, but Father Bucali immediately shut me down, dismissing it quickly with an angry reply in Romanian, pointing back down the road and concluding his words with a repetition of what he had said — but this time in English for my benefit: "Go, go, only those two, I am busy, go." Then, turning around, he took his leave and walked back into the church to resume where he had left off with the altar boys.

As we were leaving the church grounds, the craftsman, who had heard the part of the conversation in Romanian, followed after us. Looking at me and then Petr, he spoke with his finger pointing back at the church. Petr translated what he was saying. The

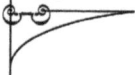

third vampire was buried in a cemetery at the back of the church. This cemetery was only used by the clergy for the burial of priests and belonged to the church. We couldn't see behind the church from where we were standing, so we walked down a side road that ran alongside the right side of the church, where the rectory was located. Once we got beyond a tall perimeter hedge that had obscured our sight, the rear of the church was partially visible through the hedge. Then the hedge stopped and became an old, moss-covered wall. This walled section of the grounds concealed the graveyard. Upon pulling ourselves up onto the wall to peek over it, we could see several slabbed headstones standing upright and a few high crosses used as headstones. I inquired as to where the third corpse was buried. After consulting with the craftsman, "Right there," Petr said. We were right above it.

This one grave was enclosed by a wrought iron fence made of daisy-chained crucifixes, which completely surrounded the grave on all sides even though the wall cornered two sides of the grave site. I gave the craftsman a few Romanian Lei for his help, and then Petr and I walked across to the magistrate's office to request permission to exhume the dead. Mr. Enache gave his blessing if we had the approval of the Church, which meant we could only exhume the two corpses in the cemetery on the outskirts of town. The Church wielded greater power in these parts than elected officials, so we couldn't get permission to exhume the corpse buried on church grounds. Petr and I then left to find and hire a few laborers for the following day.

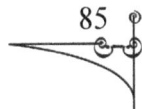

The next morning was a clear day, though the ground was wet from showers throughout the night. The air was fresh as breaks in the clouds allowed the sun to shine through on and off. Father Bucali and two men accompanied Petr and me to the cemetery; one carried shovels and a pickaxe, and the other carried a flat board on which to lay the body. I carried my bag of tools, while Petr carried two rolled-up cloths to remove the corpse.

Once there, the priest showed us to the grave Dr. Kelly had exhumed, so we left that one untouched. Exhumation began on the grave next to it, on the right. This grave held a young girl who had died four or five years ago, and no headstone existed to detail her name, birth, or death. We were able to prop the board up with one end resting on a rectangular headstone close by and the other end resting on wooden stilts retrieved from a caretaker's shed at the entrance of the cemetery. After digging for a few hours, we reached a flimsy coffin, which disintegrated as we tried to move it. Using two long cloths rolled in from both sides to meet in the middle and a long, narrow plank of wood, we were able to gently roll the corpse on its side. We then positioned the cloths, unrolled them a bit, and put the plank lying down in place. Then we gently rolled the corpse back over onto the items and onto her other side as the cloth was unrolled further. The body was returned to the supine position. The plank of wood between the cloths and the corpse gave it support from head to foot. Grabbing the cloth ends, four of us lifted her out and gently onto the board.

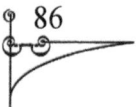

Expecting to find just bones, I saw that her flesh wasn't completely decomposed. It was dried out like leather but still very much intact, as if mummified. She had a large, flat, tapered stone shoved into her mouth, which I removed, causing Father Bucali to sigh loudly, step back, and raise his crucifix for protection. The stone was a common burial practice for those considered vampires to prevent biting. Her hair color was ginger, so I inquired if this was her natural color. Father Bucali nodded yes but also indicated that the color had faded and now was lighter and not as vibrant as when she was alive. The young girl had died in a fall while playing with friends on a large boulder they would often climb. Her head wound was still visible on the side of her head. Her hair, matted with blood, had become fused with her skin during decomposition. When I pushed in on the now blackened area, it gave way, indicating the skull had been broken in this area, probably from the fall and likely the cause of death. The rest of her skull was still firm bone. I examined her teeth, arms, hands, legs, and feet, finding nothing unusual.

Apart from her red hair, which I already knew was one superstitious qualifier for a vampire, I asked if any other abnormalities made her one. Father Bucali tapped the middle of his chest, prompting me to look there. A dried-out, brittle dress still clothed the girl, and out of respect, I had not looked beneath it at her neckline. I began removing partial fragments of her dress, which began tearing as I tried to unbutton it. On her leathery grey skin, there was a dark circle with a small protrusion at the center, just to the left of her

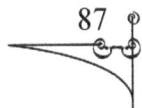

sternum, above her left breast. It looked like it may have been a third nipple. Pointing to it, I turned to the priest, and he confirmed with a nod. If one qualifier wasn't bad enough, two most certainly doomed this poor girl to a life of ridicule and mental anguish. Beyond this, there was nothing unusual. This was an unfortunate, though seemingly normal, young girl who had died a tragic death.

I inquired, "Is that it, were these the only features that made this girl a vampire?"

I was told, "Those, plus her unruliness and that she didn't attend church."

"Many children act unruly, and not attending church is the parents' fault, not the child's," I said, standing up and shaking my head in disbelief.

How this girl was perceived made me angry to the point of confronting the priest and scolding him with a slew of words: "Your self-righteousness is both arrogant and ignorant. There is nothing here to suggest that this corpse was anything other than a typical young girl. Red hair is not an evil peculiarity, and many people are born with defects or birthmarks. Didn't King David have red hair and yet was loved by God, and didn't Jacob walk with a limp after being touched by an angel? If I was to examine you, I'd probably find a defect. Look!" As I rolled up my sleeve to expose a birthmark on my forearm, I continued, "So should we start labeling everyone with a defect or those different to us as a witch or a vampire? Damn it, I mean, doesn't Scripture tell us that we all fell from perfection and that Christ died to redeem us?"

I wanted to say more but stopped short. One of my many flaws was my hot head and quick temper. Though seldom pushed to that point, I was unusually irritable that day. I tried to temper it with logic, but reasonableness and self-control are sometimes lost in the heat of the moment. Father Bucali couldn't believe anyone would address him this way. He didn't have to say anything; I could just sense it by the way he stared at me. I immediately regretted my sharp outburst, bowed my head, and shook it, saying, "I'm sorry, that was very disrespectful of me."

"Yes it was," he replied and continued, "Some people are beyond redemption, and Scripture also acknowledges the presence of evil in the world. So perhaps you are also from the sons of darkness," he snarled as he turned and abruptly walked away. I raised my head up to the sky, inhaled deeply, and took a brisk walk around the cemetery to cool off. We then finished up, returned the body to its resting place, buried the young girl, and paid the workers. Once back in town, I needed to file a report of the exhumation for the town records as Dr. Kelly had.

It was now early afternoon, so Petr and I took our lunch while I jotted down notes in my journal. My mind was now focused on that third corpse buried on church grounds. I felt that was the one worth pursuing despite not having permission to do so. Father Bucali's abrupt dismissal regarding this corpse made me curious, and the fact it was buried on holy ground also had me wondering. I needed to exhume this corpse but would most likely have to do it illegally and in secret. I doubted he would ever give me

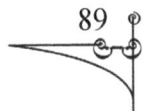

the time of day again after the way I had so insolently treated him. I inquired about his schedule over the next week and found out that on the following Monday, he needed to attend an informal meeting with the priest of a neighboring parish that would have him away from his church for the best part of the day. I decided to take my chances then. It had taken two men approximately two hours to exhume the young girl, so perhaps I could do this one alone in four. I didn't want to involve Petr out of fear of us being caught and him getting into trouble. Father Bucali's journey was at least three hours one way by carriage, and I figured he'd be there at least two hours before returning, giving me at least an eight-hour window.

Monday came and as planned; the priest left a little after daybreak as I lay in wait by the wall at the side of the church beyond the rectory. I watched as he left the rectory with a bag in hand, climbed up into the carriage, and began his journey. As soon as they rode off, I threw a shovel, a pickaxe, and my bag over the wall. I then scaled it. The seven-foot wall and hedge enclosing the cemetery gave me complete privacy. There, I removed my jacket, hanging it on the crossbeam of a high cross. I placed my bag under it, rolled up my sleeves, and went to work.

The crossed fence surrounding the grave had a hinged gate, which I opened and entered. I was careful when removing the top layer to keep the sods of grass intact so they could be replaced to make the grave look undisturbed, not that this graveyard ever got visitors. Knowing the small window of time I had to work with, I began digging with great ur-

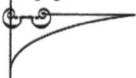

gency. Within an hour, my shirt was drenched with sweat, and beads of it streamed down my face and dripped from my dark hair. As quick as I could wipe my brow, the sweat just kept on rolling. It caused me more discomfort than any physical pain I had from digging. Adrenalin seemed to be fueling my body, and just after the third hour, I struck wood. I was surprised to see that the wood on this much older grave had not rotted. The coffin wasn't a traditional one but one roughly constructed. It resembled a sturdy wooden crate used to transport large heavy objects or weapons. I dug a clearing around the coffin so I could stand with one foot on either side of it while removing the top. Using a dagger, I was easily able to pry the lid free since the nails had rusted thin and had loosened their grip that once locked the lid in place.

Upon removing the lid, I was confronted by a skeleton that was laid face down in the prone position. No clothing existed, which meant it had been buried naked. At first glance it looked like just another human skeleton until my eyes noticed the posterior aspect of the appendicular skeleton, in particular the shoulder girdle with scapula. It was remarkably similar to the one I had been shown at the manor in County Meath, except now I had a complete specimen to examine. Before getting out of the grave to retrieve my bag, I noticed that the limbs had been shackled to the bottom of the crate-like coffin in such a tight fashion that they had snapped the bones where they made contact at the humeri and femora. Someone had gone to great lengths to secure this creature from ever moving.

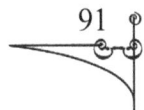

After grabbing my bag, I wiped my sweaty hands off with a small hand towel and then spread it out on the ground next to the grave, which was at chest level as I was standing in the grave. I placed my journal on the towel, opened it, and began taking notes and sketching anatomical features. The hands and feet had been amputated and were not present. I lifted the skull and turned it up to examine it, but it just looked exactly like a human skull. The only anomaly was that the lateral incisors, teeth numbers 7 and 10, were missing. There was also a one-inch hole at the front and rear of the skull, as if a pole or weapon of some sort had been forced through the skull. The pelvis area indicated that the creature's sex might be female, though this method is not always an accurate gauge of gender. Then I stooped down to examine the scapula again.

Both shoulder blades consisted of two parts laterally joined. The humerus fit into a ball and socket joint as in humans. However, with these scapulae split into two parts, a lesser scapula then fit into a greater scapula via another ball and socket joint. This was nothing like anything seen in humans. Between these scapulae, however, on both sides, was another long bone protruding that was a half-ball with a crater, as if the lesser scapula fit into it and then these bones fit into the joint of the greater scapula. It was thinner than the arm's humerus but completely severed close to the bone's head by a sharp instrument on both sides of the skeleton. I was able to fit all three pieces together on one side and move this bone in its socket to approximate its range of motion. My only

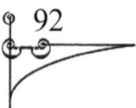

conclusion was that these were additional limbs, like the partial humeri of wings that had been deliberately removed. The thoracic cage also showed signs of violence, with several broken ribs on both sides, including bone scars from a sharp metal object being forced through the rib cage from one side and out the other side.

By now I had several pages of notes and drawings in my journal but had lost track of time. I checked the pocket watch in my jacket; it was already past two. With his meeting having been around noon, Father Bucali was probably already on his way back. Part of me wanted to keep the stub of the wing humerus, but grave robbing was a serious crime, so I dared not. I made one last inspection of the skeleton before returning the lid and then began frantically shoveling the dirt back into the grave. The grass sod sections finally concealed the freshly dug dirt and gave the grave that untouched look from a distance.

That evening, while reviewing my notes to see if I had missed anything, my mind began wandering. I pulled out a book I had brought with me on the anatomy of flyers and began studying it. I was specifically interested in the shoulder girdle of birds and bats. I had no material on prehistoric flyers to consult to see if larger extinct flyers had shown a different anatomical construct to modern flyers since they needed to support greater weight. However, the one issue I kept running into was the fact that birds, bats, and even pterosaurs only required the skeleton and muscles to support a single set of wings. The shoulder girdle of this creature needed to support the opposing

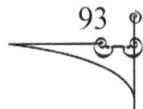

movement of both wings and arms, so perhaps no reference material would suffice. This anatomy was unique, and I was, therefore, at a loss.

It was the next Tuesday when Petr and I returned from a long hike. Famished, we went to the inn for a meal, and while there, we got news of a boy from a neighboring town who had gone missing while hiking with a friend. The town was on the other side of the mountain pass. Tragic though it was, it piqued my interest when I heard the events surrounding it. I needed to meet this boy's friend, and after asking around, I found a local man who was willing to take us there the following day for a small fee, which I gladly paid. The journey took us through Prahova Valley and a pass that went right through the mountains and onto the slopes of the other side. Azuga was a few hours from Bucegi and nestled in the mountains. The boy's friend was sleeping, suffering from shock. He was placed in the care of a physician and family when we arrived, and as a result, we were unable to see him at that time. Some locals had already formed a search party and were at the summit looking for the missing boy, so we followed as others started up the slope to join in the search. The hike wasn't nearly as strenuous as the ones Petr and I had acclimated to. It was a more gradual slope, and one found themselves on the flat summit without really knowing it until one walked to the west end of it, where it suddenly dropped off without warning. We found ourselves with a complete 360-degree view of the surrounding area. The edge of the cliff overlooked the same passage

Petr and I had hiked in but from the other side of the mountain. We had never gone all the way through; it was over a day's hike, and one could only hike so far if one was to return to town before darkness fell. It wasn't the darkness that scared me, but the dangers involved in being lost and exposed to the elements concerned me more for Petr's sake. Without adequate mountaineering supplies, nights were cold at these elevations, even during the summer months.

We were shown the area where the boy had gone over the side. The only evidence seemed to be disturbed lichen, which had been scraped and torn from the granite by a weight dragged across it in a direction that was diagonal to the edge of the cliff but would still bring the same fate. Following this diagonal brought us to the edge where a local was lying, holding a rope. Peering over the edge, there wasn't a straight line of sight. The rock face jutted out about twenty-five feet below, but the fall looked like a five-hundred-foot fall in total. The local holding a rope had a horseshoe and a white rag tied to its end, so it served as a marker for those searching below. What was strange was the boy's body had not been found below. There was no blood or any other visible evidence to suggest he had even fallen to his death.

That gave me hope that the boy was still alive; however, to the locals, it was an even worse sign, one involving their superstitions. A boy falling off this edge, if he hadn't cleared the sloping rock face below due to sheer momentum, would have at least bounced off it, and his body would still have landed in the same vicinity below, but nothing. On

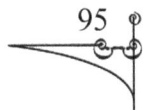

speaking to some of the locals who had heard about the events, I learned that the boys would normally have been home while it was still light, but they had lost track of time while playing at a lake farther northeast. According to one local, dusk had already begun, prompting the boys to return home. Markus and Radu were their names, and they knew this mountain well and had been racing home. Markus, the older of the two and taller, was about thirty feet ahead when he heard a screech from behind. He couldn't tell whether the screech was from Radu or something else, but he turned only to see the white of Radu's shirt as he went over the edge, though only a portion of his shirt was visible, as if something darker before him blocked complete visibility. Markus also noticed that when Radu went over the edge, he appeared to be in an upright position but moving in a direction opposite to the one they were heading in. Markus thought he had felt a stiff rush of air over his head right before the incident, but everything had happened so quickly and in near darkness that he couldn't really be sure about anything. We spent that night in the town, as I wanted to revisit the mountaintop the following day.

That evening began weeping, and the rains came as if the sky was mourning the loss of innocence. The following morning the saturated clouds had not emptied, and the sky continued to look ominous in all directions throughout the day. Petr and I decided to take a carriage back to Bucegi and return when the rains had abated. The rains held their strength for a week, and there was nothing else

to do other than settle in with the locals and converse or read. Bucegi had a small store which sold all sorts of knickknacks, including books. All were in Romanian, but out of tedium, I was happy to work my way through the shelves, flicking through each book in the hope of finding at least pictures or some other visuals to overcome my ennui. I came across a yellow jacketed book with red typography which I pulled off the shelf, and I was surprised to find it was a copy of Bram Stoker's *Dracula*. I didn't think that such books would travel this far so soon, but I guessed that because the subject matter was close to Romania's culture, this was one of the few books that had reached Romania with accelerated access.

The few books I had brought with me I had already read, and since I couldn't communicate, my only other alternative was a game of chess, which I occasionally played at the inn. I asked Petr about the book and if he could translate while reading, which wasn't a problem for this bright young lad. I had become quite keen on Petr. He was quiet, unimposing, though inquisitive. I hardly noticed his presence sometimes, and I had started mentoring him in my field and with the books I had brought. His mind was well able for anything I could throw at him, and so I didn't see any reason why such a sharp mind should be left idle. I bought a copy of *Dracula*. It seemed like the perfect occasion for such a read, though the duration of the read fell far short of that of the rains. Stoker had spent eight years of his life researching and writing his masterpiece. After reading and translating the book for me, Petr read it

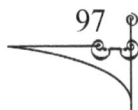

again. I let him keep it and wrote my address on the inside cover for him to stay in correspondence with me.

A week later, we returned to Azuga. The rains had stopped there a few days earlier than in Bucegi. I reasoned that if the boy had gone over the side but wasn't found below, he must be somewhere in between unless he simply didn't go over the side. I walked along the edge where he had gone over. The sparse growth was still disturbed, and I continued walking for approximately forty feet until the edge began to slope outwards so that I could see the rock face below me. There was a ledge about thirty feet below that looked level and wide enough to support me. The fifty-foot length of rope I had brought I tied around myself, anchoring it to a large pillar of rock that rose a few feet vertically. It would have been too rounded were it not for a vein of softer rock that had eroded away, allowing the rope to slide down between it. I had Petr watch the knot and stay put for fear I should get myself into trouble. The rope was knotted at regular intervals while also fastened around me. Backing up over the edge scared me, and so I found some holds that enabled me to climb down while using the rope only as a safety measure. My descent was slow as my feet blindly searched for rests to place my weight on, but I felt good knowing that climbing back up would be easier.

Upon reaching the ledge below, I found it wider than anticipated, as it was partially hidden from sight above. Part of its wall sloped inwards and was overhanging, but only to about five feet above the

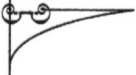

ledge itself. This meant that I could stand upright on the ledge, but the sloping wall pushed me to its edge, giving me only eighteen inches or so to work with, too close for comfort. If I hunkered down, the ledge offered me approximately three feet. My movement would be slower, but I opted for the safer method as I would have to remove the rope from around my waist regardless, and mountaineering was not a skill I had or was likely to develop any time soon. We had thrown another rope over the edge where Radu was believed to have plummeted. It acted as a marker for me, as I couldn't see the top anymore from my now hidden vantage point. I could not see the rope either from where I was, indicating the ledge I was on pushed outwards and around, a bend I would have to traverse. As I pushed towards it, the ceiling of the overhanging wall got lower until I was forced to crawl on my stomach. Nearing the bend, I was still supported by the ledge, but it was narrow.

My neck could now be extended out from the ledge to the point that I could see the marker, a free-hanging piece of rope, but the rock face behind it, the overhanging escarpment, recessed back into the cliff and was still hidden from me. I would have to leave the safety of the ledge to traverse around the jutting corner. Below me, the face again sloped outwards, and the ledge offered enough holds for my immature skills to feel secure enough.

Once off the ledge, I began to traverse around it. On rounding the corner, I got the distinct whiff of decomposing flesh, pungent enough to indicate it was something large. My eyes started scanning

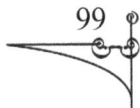

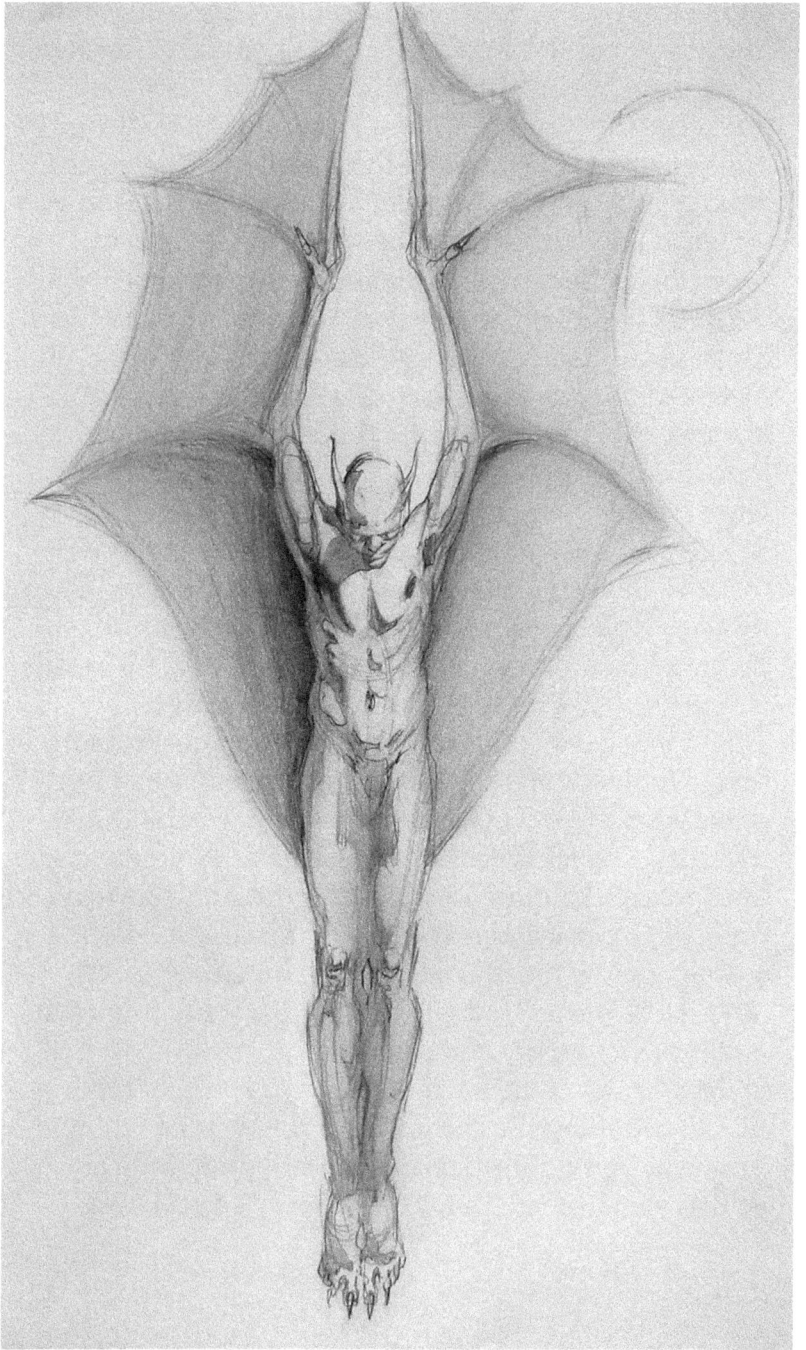

and following my nose as I tried to hone in on the direction the smell was coming from. My eyes were also deceived into searching for the bright colors of clothing against this sea of greyness. After all, this surely was the smell of Radu's body. A careless movement made in haste to locate the source caused my foot to slip, and so I was quickly reminded of the peril around me. I composed myself and again resorted to slow, deliberate movements, which brought me safely around the corner and back onto the safety of the ledge.

The ledge then widened further, cutting into the cliff face, deeply so. It seemed to open into the cliff like a cave, and darkness prevailed within, but the overhanging ceiling became too low for me even to attempt to crawl in. The odor of rotting flesh was now starting to turn my stomach. What was dead was right before me, judging from the intensity of the smell, but my eyes were still deceived because I was imagining a white shirt and brown slacks grabbing my attention.

Then I saw what looked like a yellowish-grey claw. Before I could figure that out, the one claw became five, with the others hidden in line behind the one I was seeing, but the flesh was grey, the color of the surrounding rock perfectly camouflaged. Removing a handkerchief from my pocket, I used it to grab hold of what I suspected was an eagle's talons. I pulled the creature from the darkness of this cavern and into the light of day. Its dead weight caused my heart to jump with fright. This was something other than an eagle. I had seen golden eagles before, some

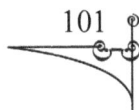

of the largest birds of prey, but this was far larger.

As I pulled, the body revealed itself, and even as my eyes adjusted, the head came into sight. There was still something larger trailing it. The underarm showed a fold of skin stretching backwards under and beyond the arms and head, a large wing. In my excitement, I began doubting what I was seeing, and a thousand thoughts collected and collided in my mind. Had I wronged someone who hated me so much as to play such a wild and extravagant trick in order to discredit me? A few more moments of composure, and I realized that what I was looking at was real. Had the fable become fact?

Maggots had already begun their work. I had to return to the rope to have Petr lower my pack, which had my surgical tools and journal. Petr would have to be content with sitting for another few hours; I hoped he wouldn't mind because he was reading *Dracula* again for the third time. The ropes weren't long enough to stretch around the rock face for me to pull the corpse off the cliff's ledge, nor did we have the strength even if we could have used the ropes. I figured that where it lay was an ideal spot because it was hidden from view and out of access from scavengers save the flies. The shelf was wide enough to study the specimen, and this way, I could work now and then return later for further work before getting others involved.

I took a few moments to look at the creature before beginning work and began jotting down some notes and sketching physical characteristics, etc. Using a thin, flaked piece of rock, I first removed the maggots from the abdominal area, which had the largest infestation of them, before breaking the rigor mortise state in order to stretch out the corpse so I could take measurements. Though bloated from the buildup of gases during decomposition, the creature had an emaciated look to it. Skeletal outlines were visible, especially around the rib cage. The creature's gender was visibly female, and from crown to heel, it measured five feet seven inches, to which an inch or two could probably be added due to shrinkage and its slightly contorted position, but even at five-seven, this was several inches taller than the average human female.

The creature was human-esque, so much so that I had a hard time describing it in the zoological terms used for animals. For instance, the talons were the curved, powerful claws seen in birds of prey, but they were not completely like the talons of a carrion bird but rather in the form of hands as in humans, i.e., having opposable thumbs indicating great dexterity, something only found in primates or creatures approaching humans in dexterity or motor skills. The feet were likewise similar to human feet, but the phalanges were longer than in humans, more like fingers and therefore probably more dexterous than human feet, but also with the ball of the foot, arch, and heel indicating a bipedal functionality which was also evident by other anatomical features such as the hips and spinal column. The wingspan was approximately ten to twelve feet. A wound caused by a heavy blow to the back of the skull may have been the cause of death, and the skull had been fractured.

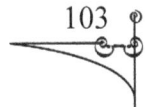

The hours seemed to vanish, and before I knew it, visibility began waning. Upon looking up, the sun had disappeared from sight and become low in the sky. I knew darkness was about to fall. I pushed the partially dissected creature back into the recess, as I felt this was as good a hiding place as any. I had amputated a digit from the hand and taken some other samples of tissue, hair, and coagulated blood. An eye would have been a good sample, but they were already in a reduced, sunken state. I nevertheless extracted one for further examination under a microscope as well as hair samples. I would return early the next day while also sending word for a photographer in Bucharest. I felt the world wasn't ready, and I needed physical proof other than my notes if, for some reason, I couldn't remove the corpse for further study. Petr had fallen asleep during my investigation, thankfully so. I was sorry to have kept him waiting, and had the perils of the creature's location not been so great, I would have had him help. I withheld the find from him, as he was young and excitable and would surely have told others before I wanted others involved, and we hurried back to the village.

I found it hard to sleep that night. My mind was too active, racing, piecing the puzzle together while letting my imagination get the better of me with what-ifs. I eventually succumbed to the needs of my body and dozed off. The following morning, it was the sound of torrential rain pounding the roof and windows that woke me from my slumber. I hadn't counted on this. Yesterday had appeared fine and

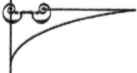

cloudless, but today, I couldn't return, which upset me greatly. I decided that I would get more rope and pull the creature from the cliff. My only problem with this, of course, was that word would get out, and my peaceful study would be interrupted. Trying to conceal the corpse would probably make matters worse since it could be perceived by others that it was Radu's body. The fact that we had not found his body still vexed me.

The rain, torrential at times, didn't let up for three days and three nights. Though far from mundane, I was confined to the limits of my small community. I studied the samples I had taken by day, which offered the best light even with overcast skies and bursting clouds. With the few books I had access to, I therefore took to sketching and refining my notes, researching the anatomical features of like animals found in nature and then speculating on what I had discovered in an attempt to build a physiological composition of this unique creature.

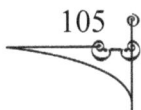

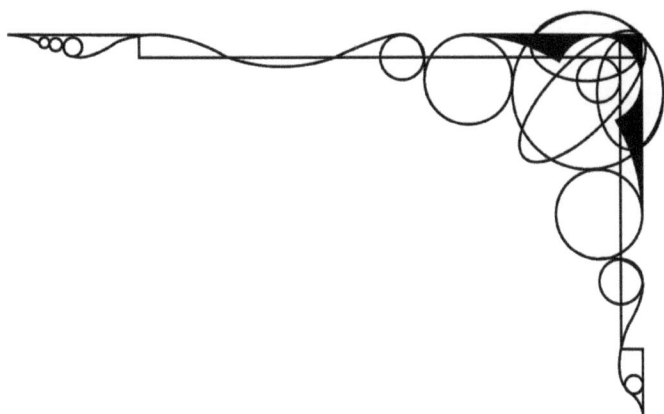

Venous heme in darkness flows
Electrum sun with livid lips
Piercing tooth my craving grows
Ferrous kiss drains my heart
beneath cold limbs of pinning hips

Physiology

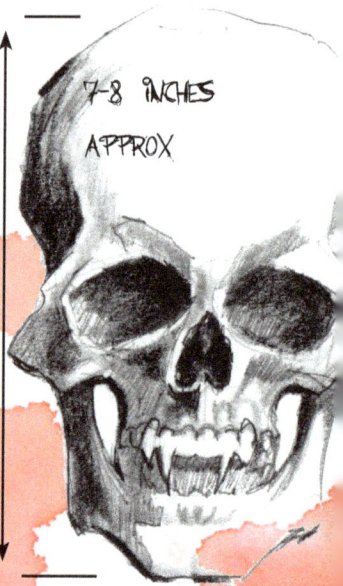

7-8 INCHES
APPROX

AUXIL

PECTORALIS MAJOR LARGER THAN IN HUMANS
HAS ORIGINS AT ANTERIOR SURFACE OF STERNUM
AND MEDIAN TO FULL PART OF CLAVICLE

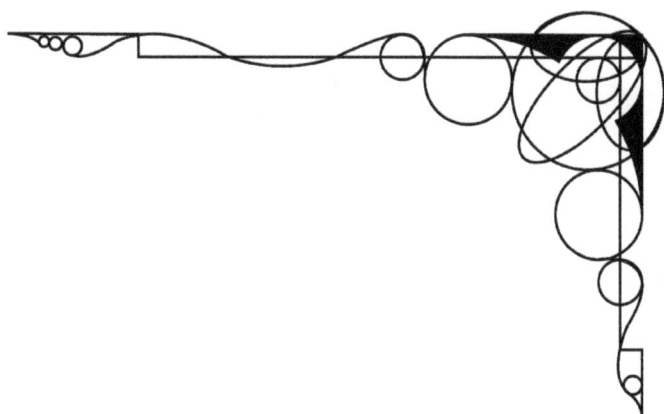

Arterial heme, vermillion glows
In passions hot with hurting touch
on naked flesh in fluid love
Laps my breath in scarlet lust
Ecstacy, a hex on me

7 - Vampire Physiology

$\mathcal{V}$ampirism in nature does exist in such forms as the vampire bat, leeches, mosquitoes, or any of the host of organisms that feast upon blood. Scientifically it is called Hematophagy, deriving from the Greek word for blood (*haima*) and eat (*phagein*). Blood is a fluid food rich in nutrients, namely proteins and lipids, and can be accessed with minimum effort and in bountiful supply. Thus, hematophagy has become a preferred form of feeding in many small animals and insects, though in humans it is considered a psychological sickness.

Vampires seem to have lived alongside humans and have dwelled amongst us since the dawn of our existence. Stories from various cultures across the globe and scant evidence in Mesopotamia exist to support that conclusion. Other evidence can be derived from deductive reasoning, for example, the fact that their whole demeanor has evolved to mimic human form, to assimilate and blend, though their natural state shows distinct anatomical differences. Although not immortal, their lifespan may be consider-

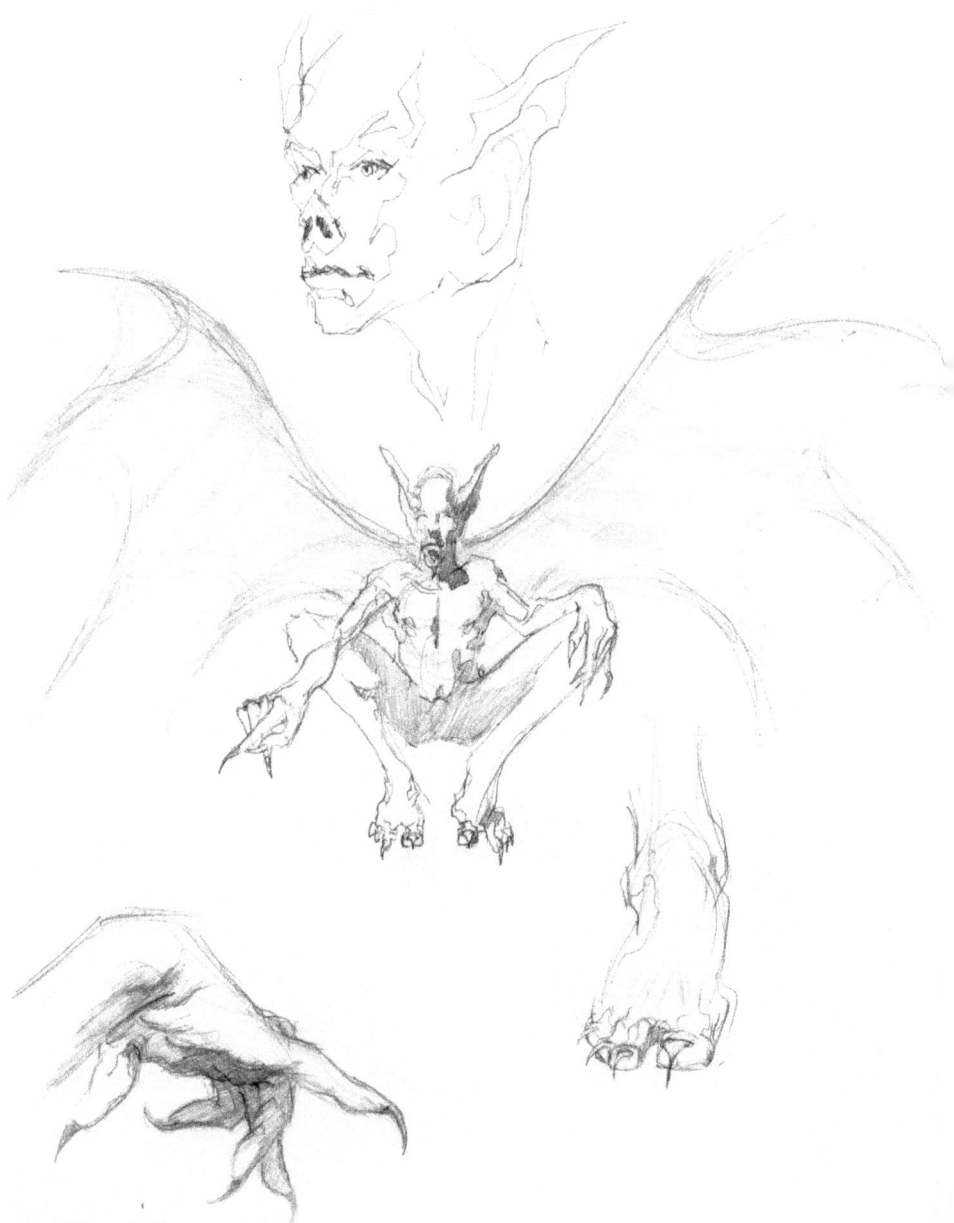

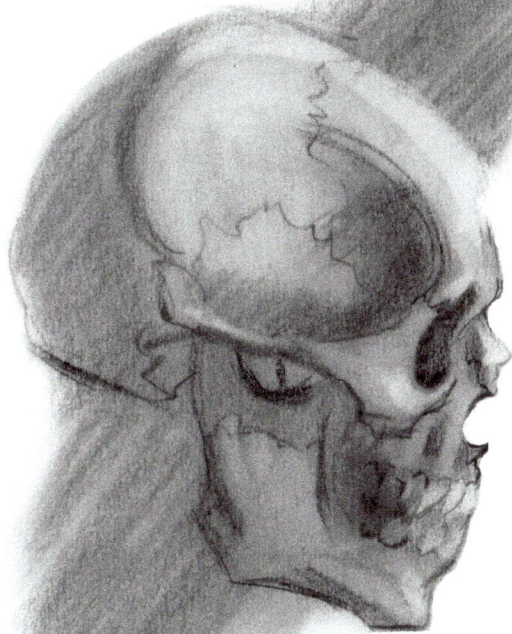

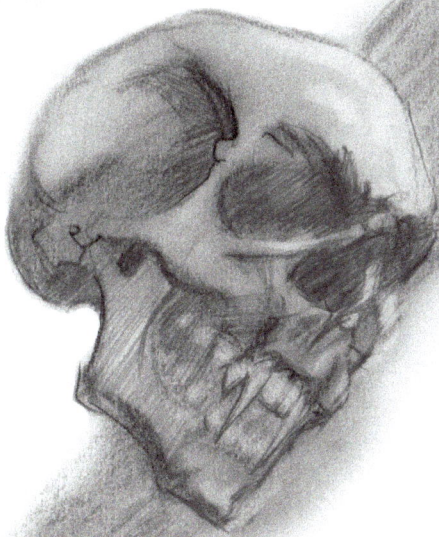

Invasive position?

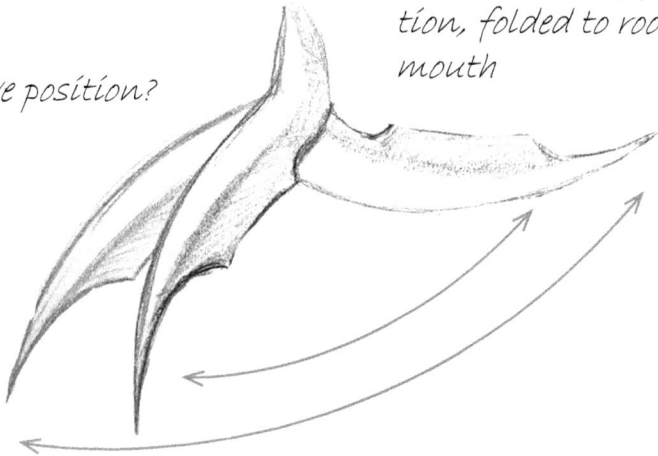

Normal resting position, folded to roof of mouth

Aggressive/defensive position?

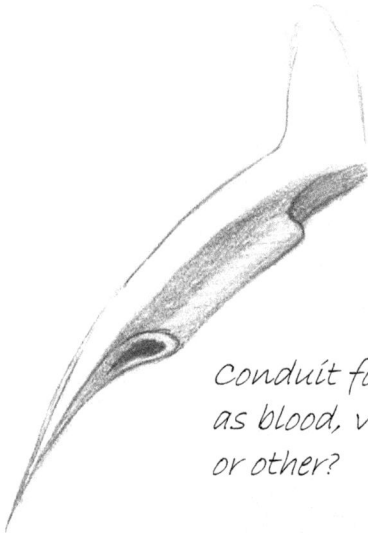

Conduit for fluids such as blood, venom, saliva, or other?

ably longer than that of humans but is unknown at present. Given this fact, and with a brain size equivalent to that of humans, it would make them of superior intelligence, which would help explain their anonymity and elusiveness. Can vampires survive on the blood of most mammals? Is human blood preferred—a preference that may be likened to why we have preferences in the type of meat we like or our choice in wine? Humans may also be preferred because they are easier prey: the price we have paid for relying on intelligence offsetting raw strength and instinct. When compared to the strength and instinct of other mammals of equivalent mass, we are slower and more easily accessible, with poor defenses. Our skin is also comparatively cleaner and thinner, with a rich supply of superficial blood in well-exposed areas such as the neck, wrist, and thighs, depending upon attire.

Mandible and Dental:

A vampire's puncturing teeth are not the cuspids (6 and 11 in humans) as generally held. They are simply too lateral to be effective. Rather, these canines, though generally larger than in humans, can be used to facilitate holding prey while the lateral incisors (7 and 10 in humans) fold out, extending via a knuckle to puncture the epidermis. Prey is normally dormant as a preferred feeding state, and therefore, no biting generally occurs. Infrared sensors in the nose locate an area where blood flows closest to the surface. Licking the area, as observed in the bat Desmodus Rotundus (vampire bat), may not only clean and soften the area but perhaps secrete a mild anesthetic so that the small needle pricks of the teeth are not even felt by the dormant

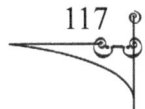

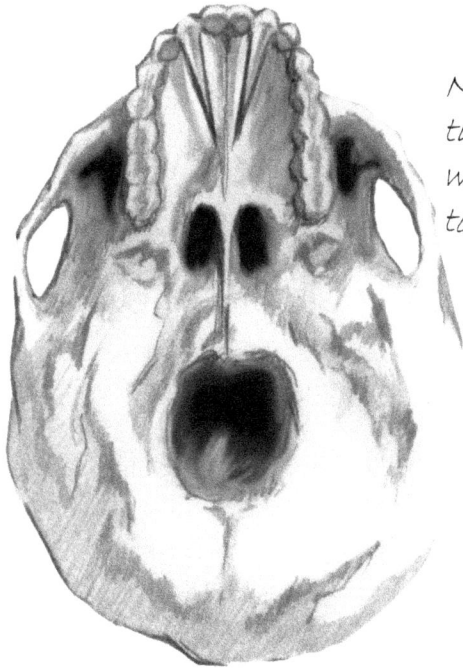

Normal resting po
tion. Fangs fold in
wards and upward
to roof of mouth

Fully extended feed
ing or defensive
position allows jaw
positioning withou
strenuous effort

prey. These lateral incisors (teeth 7 and 10 in humans) appear as teeth when mimicking but are, in fact, white cartilage, hinged and able to fold backwards up into the roof of the mouth, similar to the methodology of a viper's biting technique. These articulated teeth hold a trocar-like or hollowed enamel (solenoglyphous) fang at the end. This triangular tapered fang maximizes smooth tissue laceration, whereby there is a transfer of body fluids through hollows above and behind the tip of the fangs, opening into the roof of the mouth just as one would drink through a straw. But are these teeth used for extraction or injection—or perhaps both? In the case of a viper, venom is injected. In bats, an anticoagulant called draculin in the saliva prevents blood from clotting until teeth are withdrawn, and this would also enable the blood to be lapped as it flows freely, which seems a more efficient alternative to sucking. Most likely molars are redundant since food, being liquid, is swallowed, not chewed.

A vampire's jaw may also have the ability to dislocate, enabling a greater clamping or biting radius, similar to that of a constrictor but for a different purpose, as a constrictor utilizes this to swallow whole food. This would call for great muscle strength powerful enough to break the neck of the prey during the initial holding bite if, indeed, the prey is awake or there is a struggle. However, if we are correct about the forwards angle of the piercing fangs, no radial biting or specialized jaw maneuvers would be necessary. Vampire bats also have the ability to transfuse liquid food in the event of another bat requiring nourishment when none is available. This strange act appears as a kissing ritual in which food is transfused orally and is something that has been observed in Desmodus Rotundus.

Fangs may also be displayed during acts of
aggression or when threatened

Sight and Vision:

Vampires are nocturnal, though they can move about by day. Though in dimly lit conditions, a vampire's pupils often appear round, they are, in fact, vertical, which, together with the horizontal eyelids, gives the vampire the ability to endure the bright light of day by strictly regulating the amount of light that penetrates the lens. The retina contains two important kinds of cells. Rods respond to very low levels of light and don't distinguish between colors. Cones need a higher level of light and come in different varieties to respond to different hues. Compared to humans, vampires have few cones but plenty of rods. That means they probably see color but not very vividly. Behavioral research in nocturnal animals indicates they probably see blue and yellow better than red and green, but color overall doesn't seem very important to them. The inability to discern red would lead us to conclude that they are drawn to blood through the body heat emitted by mammals or by scent. To a vampire, a daytime world of muddy pastels is a small price to pay for its ability to hunt prey and avoid detection at night.

To boost this ability, a vampire has a reflective layer, the tapetum lucidum, behind the retina. Any light that gets through the retina the first time also bounces back, giving rods and cones a second chance to enhance an image. Many animals have these, but in a vampire, they appear particularly dazzling, leading to erroneous superstitions about seeing in total darkness or having magically lit eyes. They reflect light back, which gives the impression of glowing, but they don't have any source of emitting their own light. An outer tinted membrane between the lid and

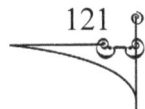

Membrane suppresses
glare

Vertical dilation of p.

eyeball can shield this reflection and suppress the glare when ambushing prey while still providing visibility. Sight may not even be necessary for capturing prey, based on their abilities to sense heat and echolocate.

Many flying creatures have the advantage of having their eyes located on the sides of their head, giving them what is called monocular vision and thus a greater spectrum of vision and awareness. In some species, 300 degrees of vision is possible without any head rotation. Vampires, however, like owls or other raptors, have forward-facing eyes (though not fixed in their sockets) and thus have binocular vision in which the spectrum of sight in both eyes overlaps. As a result, nature compensates, offering them the same agility as an owl. Human neck movement is restricted to approximately 180 degrees of rotation from one lateral extreme to the other. In vampires, however, it is approximately 270 degrees, as seen in owls. Owls give the illusion of a complete 360-degree rotation, but such freeness is impossible given the physical limits of corporeal design.

A flatter lens allows for a greater area of focus, and a larger pupil also allows for a greater collection of light in the darkness of night. Whereas humans have about 200,000 rods per square millimeter, vampires have a million or so, giving them five times the night vision of humans, and when coupled with larger pupils and the tapetum lucidum, that number greatly increases.

The foveae, which are areas of sharpness within the eye, amount to one in humans, whereas in vampires, it is two, as in other raptors. This allows for magnified sight and tight focus when flying high and searching for prey.

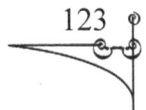

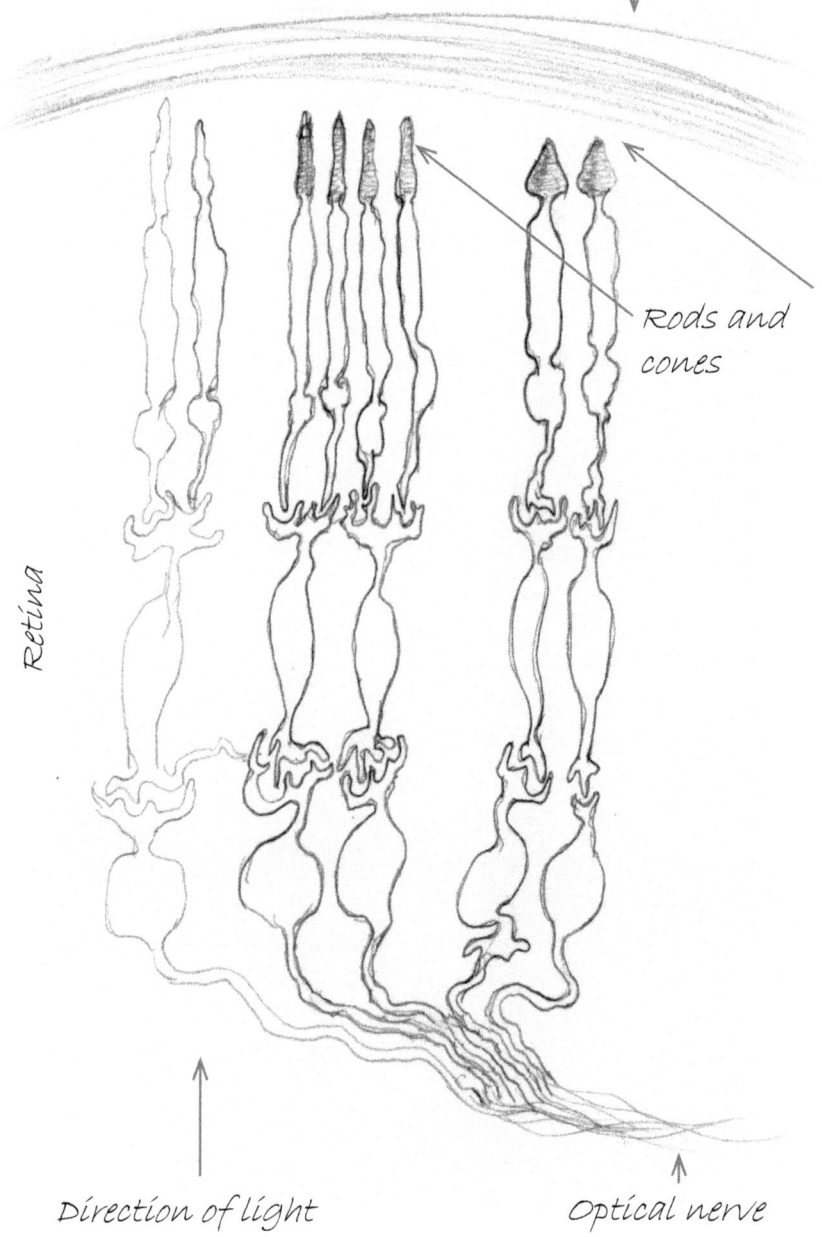

Tapetum lucidum bounces light back into the eye for a second chance and maximizes the light captured in dimly lit conditions

Rods and cones

Retina

Direction of light

Optical nerve

Skeletal Anatomy:

Vampires' skeletal construct again appears highly specialized. Rather than having bones of dense calcium, which add weight and rigidity to the human frame, and because bipedal walking isn't their only option, vampires have a similar anatomical skeletal structure with the exception that their bones appear to be composed of a material more closely related to that found in bird feathers, namely the hollow rachis, which is the central support system for each feather. This is an extremely light, flexible, but strong material made of keratin, which is a protein also used to make horns and hair in different animals and beaks in birds. This material substitutes for the denser, heavier bone composite found in humans. The probable reason for this would be to enable efficient flight, which for such a large creature may not normally be possible with the mass of our corporeal construct. Such being the case, we encounter the problem of absent bone marrow, an issue that is currently still under investigation. Bone composite, however, may still be calcium, like that found in humans, just not as dense though structurally composed to allow for flight, again an area in need of further research, some discussed in the following topic.

The Problem of Flight:

The earth's atmosphere is a delimiting factor when it comes to flight, and there are also structural limits imposed on biological fliers when it comes to anatomy, namely wingspan and body weight. Depending on how

Mimicking state, perhaps not unlike the rapid enlargement of the male phallus when stimulated, sponge-like tissue at the tips of fingers and toes fills with blood, air, or other fluid to extend digits and envelop the talons, giving the appearance of human nails and fingers.

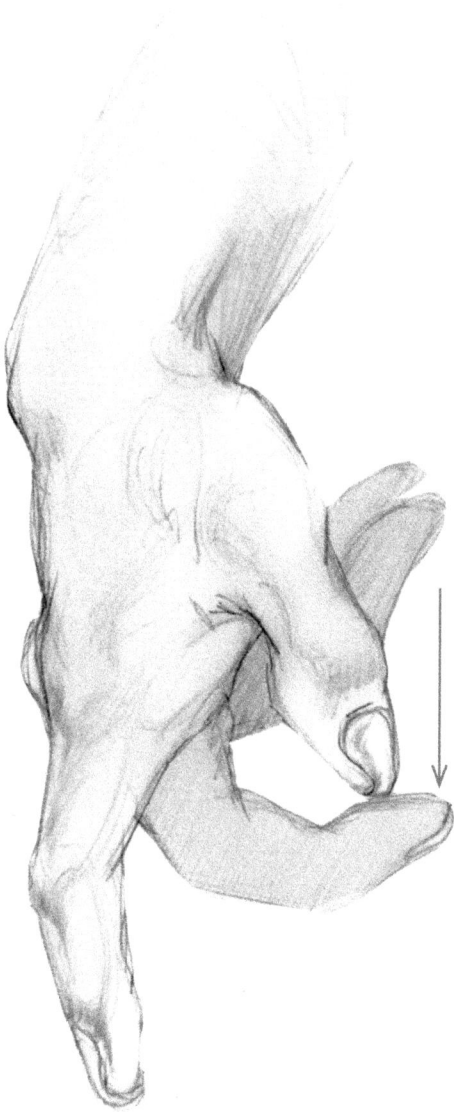

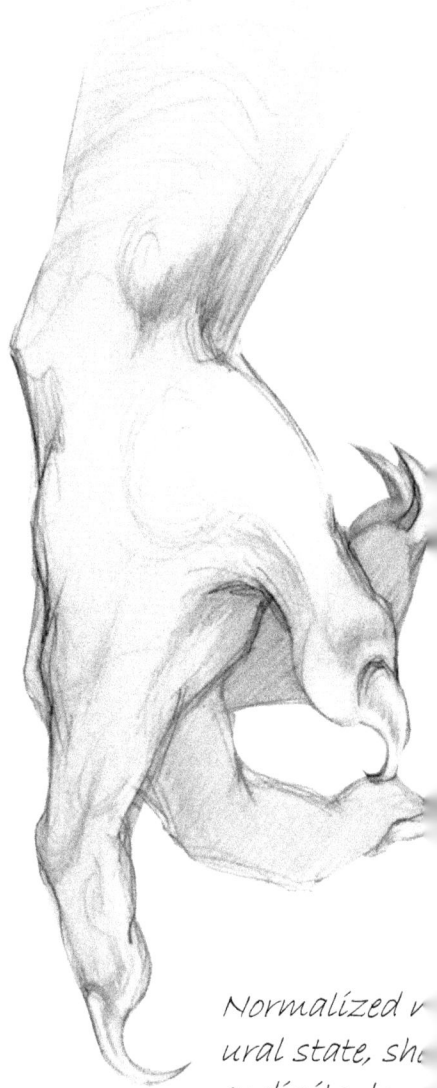

Normalized natural state, showing shorter digits, longer talons

nourishment is acquired, an effective hunter need not be of equal stature to overcome prey. The vampire bat, for example, feeds on the blood of much larger mammals such as cattle. Strength, therefore, is not required to overcome dormant prey, but stealth is. On the other hand, lions also prey on creatures larger than themselves, but such alert prey requires a greater toolset than stealth alone, such as speed, strength, and anatomical weapons like claws, fangs, and powerful jaws. Based on our source material, if we are to assume a vampire that mimics its prey, in this case, humans, its ability to blend in would give it a construct similar to ours, at least in appearance, since we are visual creatures. The height of the average human adult male in the Western world is 5'8" with the average weight being approximately 150 lb. This height and weight is subjective to race, diet, genetics, demographics, and any given period in time throughout human history, but it will suffice for our study. The human skeleton occupies about 20% of the weight of a living being.

If we assume, therefore, that a vampire (Chiroptera-sapiens or, more specifically, Homo-Desmodontidae) has an equal average height to that of a human when upright, the weight supported by its frame would most likely be less than that of a human weight for an equivalent height in order to facilitate efficient flight. A creature weighing 72 to 96 lb. would not be an unreasonable number, given that even a malnourished or slightly framed human can fall into these limits given that same height. And if, indeed, a vampire's skeleton is constructed of a different material than a human's, then even less weight would be probable. We have no such flying creatures of this size today, so should this exclude the possibility? No, in fact, we have prehis-

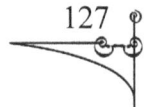

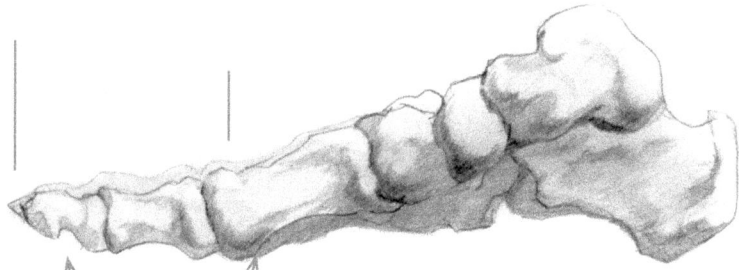

Metatarsal longer in Huma
shorter in Vampires (no cun
form)

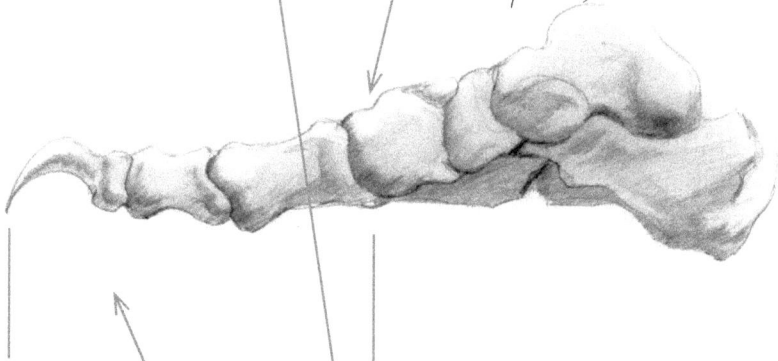

Distal Phalange, 2 in prominent toe
of human, 3 in vampire.
Phalange length closer to ratio of
digits in hand

toric fossils to help support our case. Pterosaurs and ptero-
dactyls were, at one time, a common sight in our skies of
yester-eon. Many of these flying creatures had wingspans
greater than our avians today. Even modern-day flyers like
Otis Tarda can weigh more than 40 lb. Pteranodon, discovered in 1871, had a wingspan of some 20 feet or more and
could support a weight of 110 lb., a weight within the adult
human weight range. Paleontology is still in its infancy,
and based on the massive size of some of the terrestrial
dinosaur fossils we have already discovered, we will likely
eventually discover more massive flyers capable of supporting greater weights than that of humans. The question
remains: what are the corporeal structural limits of a flyer
able to support the weight of an adult male, assuming sexual dimorphism? More discoveries and investigations need
to be made to support my assumptions.

    Adding to this, the muscle mass is smaller than
in humans and lighter when in natural form, except for
the powerful pectoral and deltoid muscles used in flight.
However, during mimicking, subcutaneous glands most
likely swell their bodies to resemble the relative bulkiness
of humans. Their digestive system is also complex, as
causing the formation of concentrated urea as water mass
would hamper flight on a full stomach. Wings are partially
attached to the proximal part of the arm but fold outwards
to the rest of the arm before locking into place at the wrist,
where the phalanges span out as in the bony ridges seen
in bats, which can be viewed as elongated webbed fingers.
Being attached to the entire arm, as in bats, would make
mimicking difficult. But being unattached completely
would make flight near impossible, and therefore partial
attachment gives the best of both worlds. This attachment

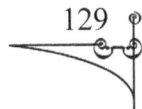

is through locking intervals along the arm, giving the wing the extra support necessary for flight in such a large creature. As in birds and extinct flying creatures such as pterosaurs, vampires have a keel on the sternum, to which the large chest muscles used for flight attach. This is a modification of the human pectoral girdle. However, in birds, the wing is supported by the main bones of the arm. A vampire wing uses a membrane of thin skin (patagium) and is essentially a webbed hand whereby the fingers support the distal area of the wing where the greatest thrust is produced. However, vampires must use their wings in conjunction with their arms to produce the strength required for flight, thus combining the methods of both avian and chiropteran flight. Though the first digit of a bat wing is small, clawed, and used for terrestrial mobility, it is not so with vampires since they are not only bipedal but have arms and hands in addition to wings. The arms of a vampire have the same bones as in humans with the exception that no ulna exists, just a radius. This ulna has become part of the wing, with a split or twin humerus, though thinner on the wing than the arm.

As arm volume decreases when returning to its natural state, the excess skin serves as the webbing membrane for a secondary wing, perhaps used for gliding. When in an upright bipedal position, the wings can then fold into the deep hollow of the back on either side of the spine. In humans, this ravine running the length of the back is caused by the surface bulk of the lumbar muscles, but in vampires, it is more pronounced so that the wings can fold into these hollows and be concealed, resulting in a smooth posterior similar to the way a beetle's wings fold into its exoskeleton. This excess skin, as a result of volume shrinkage, also happens in the gluteus area, which is necessary for stabilization in flight.

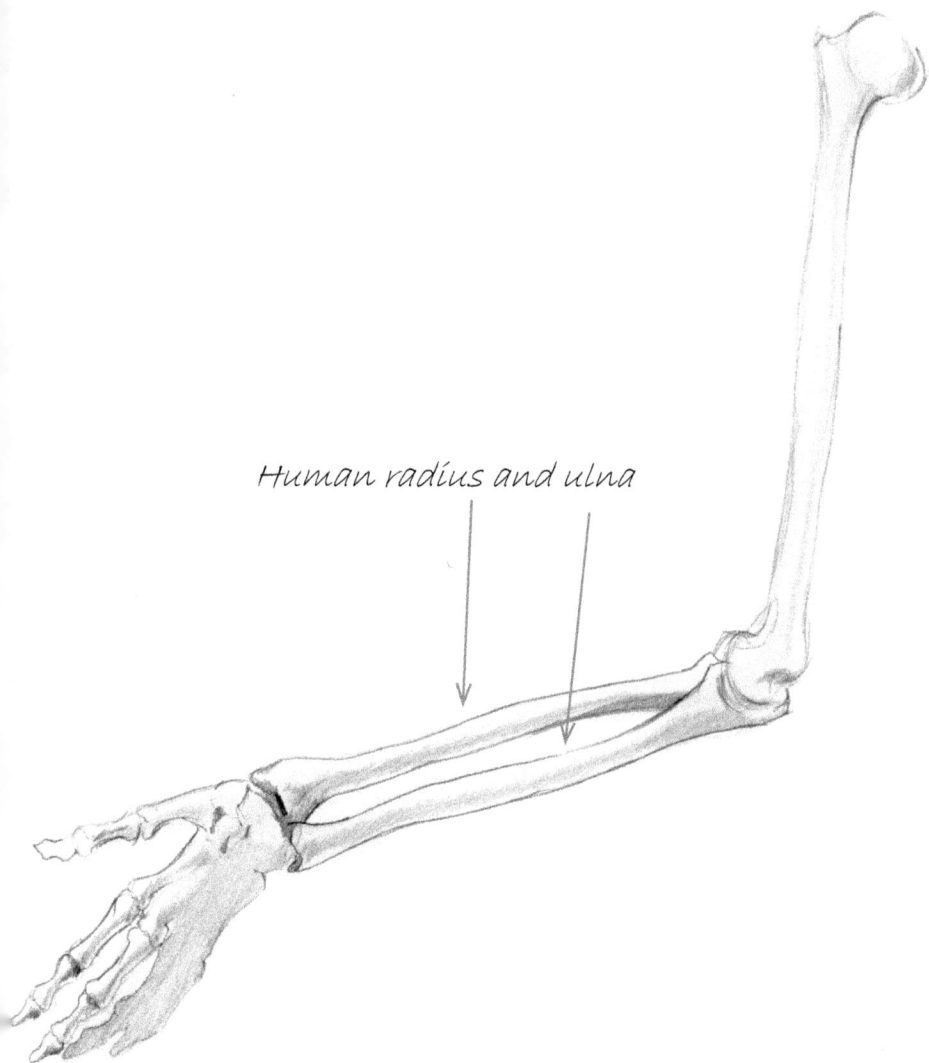

Human radius and ulna

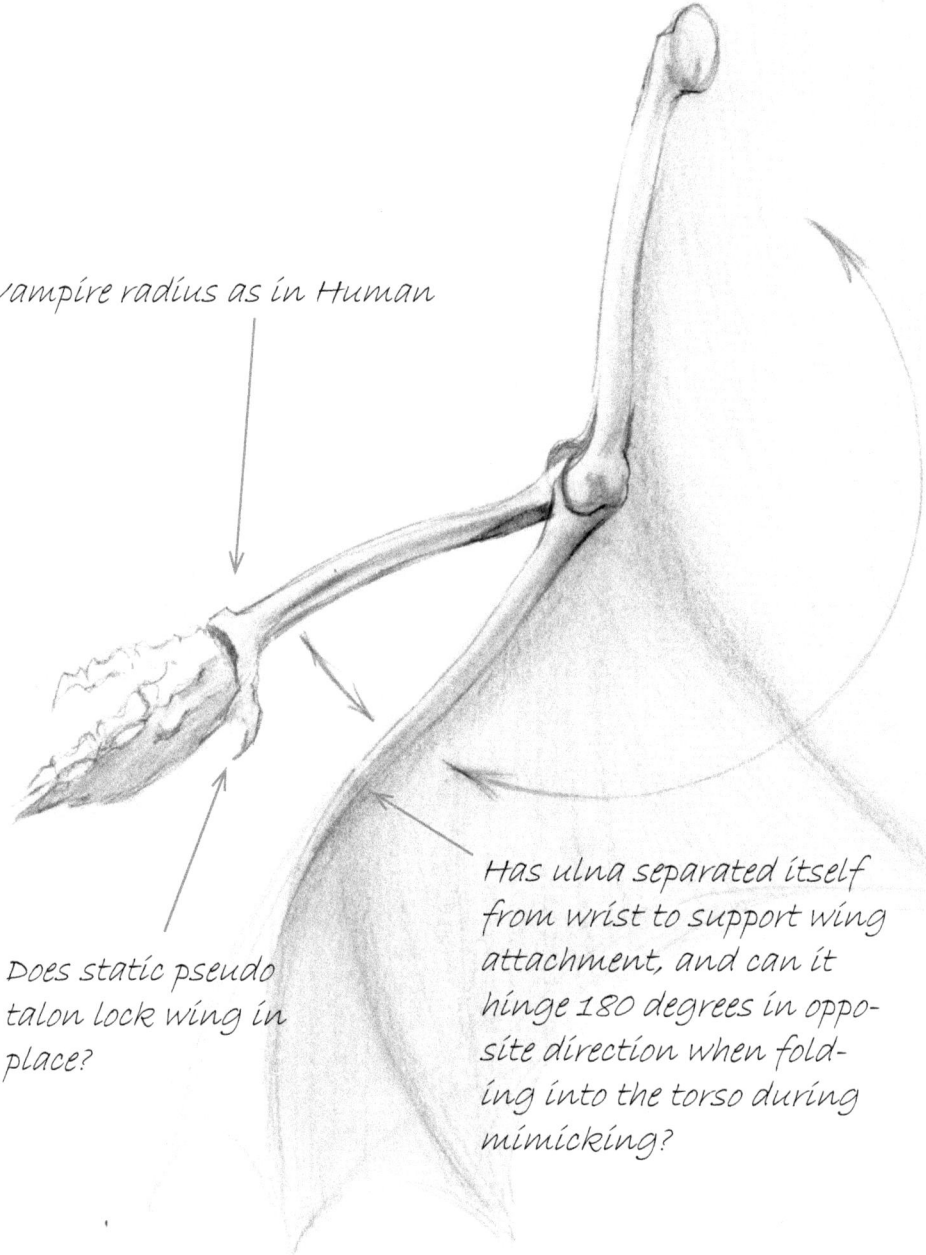

vampire radius as in Human

Does static pseudo talon lock wing in place?

Has ulna separated itself from wrist to support wing attachment, and can it hinge 180 degrees in opposite direction when folding into the torso during mimicking?

A bat wing is essentially a dis-
proportionately webbed hand

Note: perhaps wing hinges at elbow in
order to follow movement of arm but
is not attached and has its origin at
head of humerus

In natural state, it appears vampires have a fold
of skin beneath each arm which stretches from
mid underarm and attaches at boundary between
Latissimus dorsi and Sacrospinalis muscles.
Though not part of the primary wing, it may enable gliding short distances, as in flying squir-
rels, without the need to unfold primary wings.

Deep furrow in back caused by recessed
spine and tendinous planes enables wings
to be folded into back without protrusion.

Is the insertion/attachment
point here or here?

Diagram illustrates the possible folding path
wings follow. Humerus rests along Latissimus dorsi with elbow nestled into deeper plane
of sacrospinalis muscles. Ulna turns upwards
into furrow of back while digits fold downwards
along recess of spine.

Superficial Physical Attributes:

Skin color most probably shifts between a pale or ash grey to charcoal but with the ability to change and camouflage in human flesh tones. Feet appear to be prehensile, and both feet and hands contain sharp talons. Feet, though resembling human feet, are anatomically different, especially in bone length ratio. The metatarsals within the foot, which span to form the toes, are shorter in vampires than in humans, thus making the phalanges longer and more like fingers, which would enable the toes to be curled in a completely circular fashion. This ability would be a prerequisite for roosting upside down if their resting habits follow that of other chiropterans. This would most likely also add an extra phalange to the prominent toe, which in humans has only two. A vampire's talons, however, do not retract like the claws of a lion in which the claw is drawn upwards into the bulky mass of the foot by muscles. The thinness of the mimicking fingers dispels that possibility. The skin felt at the tips of the finger was loose and pliable. What most likely occurs is that in their natural state, the fleshly length of the finger is shorter, with the claw always exposed. During mimicking, bubble cells inflate, and blood, air, or other bodily fluids are sent to pouched skin at the fleshy tips, causing them to expand outwards, thus lengthening the finger while enveloping the curvature of the claw at the end. Body temperature may also be higher than in humans, accounting for greater speeds and strength, though this would also fuel a greater hunger and need to feed on a regular basis.

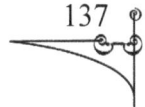

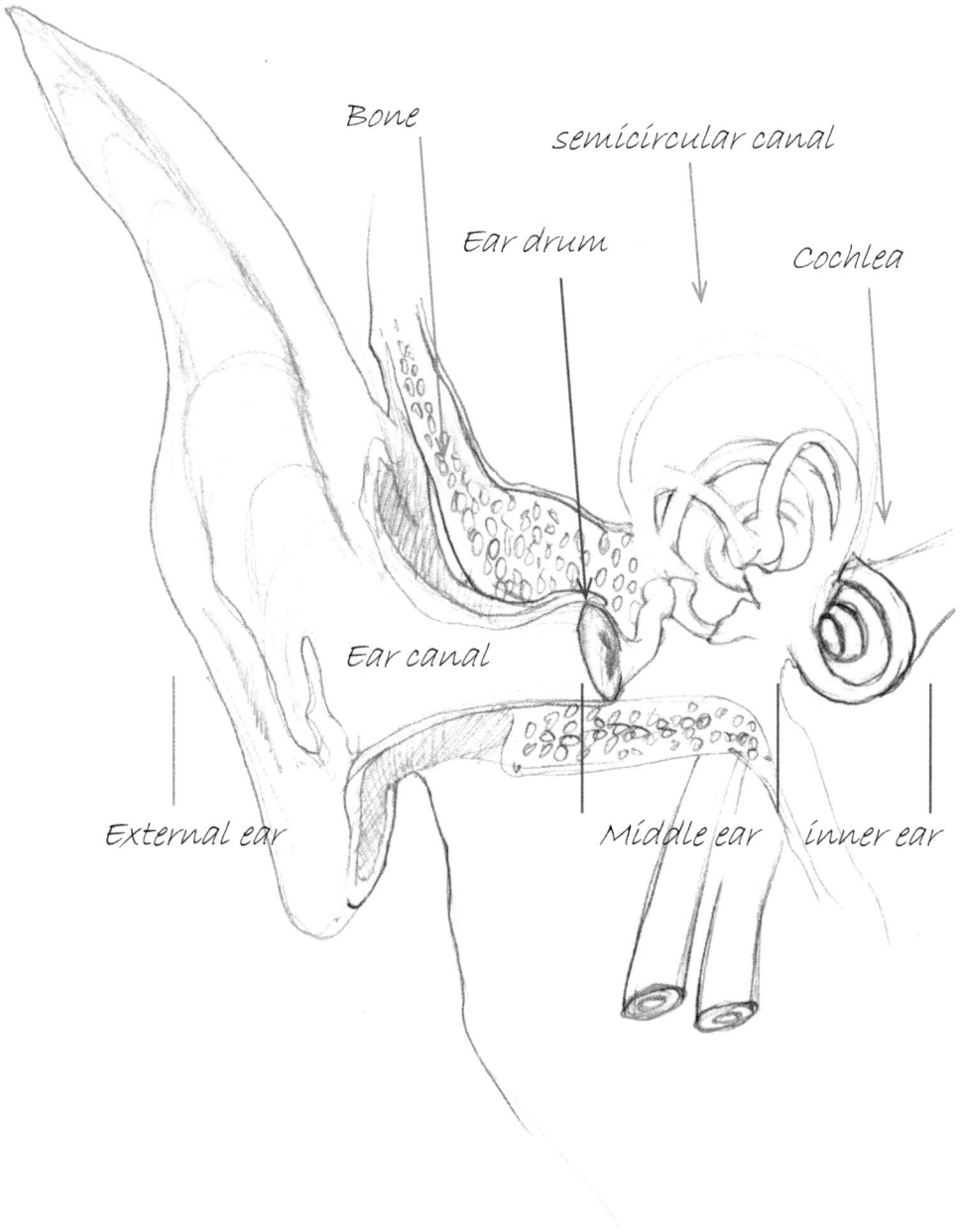

Bone

semicircular canal

Ear drum

Cochlea

Ear canal

External ear

Middle ear

inner ear

Audial and Sound

Vampires' ears most likely roll and curl in to resemble human likeness when dwelling amongst us but unfurl when blood is sent to them for echolocation in the extreme darkness of caves, where they are believed to roost. The vampire's ambiguous and elusive existence would have us conclude that they roost in the deep caverns of high cliffs and mountains, as do other bats, and most likely have an advanced navigational system. This system most likely employs the use of echolocation and would enable them to audibly see in total darkness. Whereas in mimicking form, they have the ability to communicate within human frequency ranges of 20 Hz to 20 kHz, during echolocation they shift that frequency to upwards of 30 kHz. With their brain size, they probably use a high-duty frequency cycle system in which the harmonics are also used. The frequency provides for the basics of detecting targets and measuring Doppler shifts, whereas the modulated aspect type of the pulse provides extra details. As with an echo, to explain it in familiar terms, when we shout, a sound wave is produced by the vibrating vocal cords in our neck, which resonates on air columns in the atmosphere. Air particles are pushed and transmit this energy onwards, and, as often experienced in a canyon, this sound wave bounces from the surrounding rocks and returns to us with a delay, an echo. The vampire brain works in a similar manner but with greater acuteness. What is also deciphered from the returning information is the size of the object targeted. Distance and height, even speed and direction of movement, if any, can be detected, as in bats having the ability to catch flying insects in extremely dark or low light conditions.

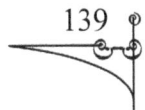

The vampire ear, when unfurled, has a span of approximately 6 to 8 inches due to its wider audible frequency range but is used only in flight, in the darkness of caves, and at night. Ridges can also be observed in the ear and act as trapping chambers. During mimicking, blood or other fluid is withdrawn from the extremities, causing the ear to lose rigidity and essentially wilt, curling inwards like a roll of paper. The ear is designed to transfer sound waves from the outside world to the brain. Sound waves are basically captured on the surface of the external ear and funneled into and through the ear canal, where they hit the eardrum, causing it to vibrate and ripple, much like those formed when a stone is dropped into a pond. These acoustics are then passed through the air-filled middle ear via the malleus, incus, and stapes (or hammer, anvil, and stirrup) to the fluid-filled inner ear, which comprises the cochlea. The inner ear also houses the semicircular canals used for balance, whose architecture is different in vampires since flight and roosting upside down give the need for a more complex sense of balance. The cochlea houses hair cells designed to collect acoustic energy through the agitation of this fluid within the inner ear. These stimulated hair cells then transfer the signals, which are converted into electrical signals and eventually deciphered by the brain. In humans, the cochlea, named for its shape, is a 2.5-turn spiral not dissimilar to the shell of a snail. However, in vampires, it is approximately four turns since there are two types of hair cells that sit side by side. One deals with the frequencies humans communicate in, and the other collects the signals from the higher frequency ranges used by bats. There is the possibility that the hair cells for the higher frequency range may be connected directly to the optic nerve in vampires,

Acromion
process

Head of
humerus

Gleniod
fossa

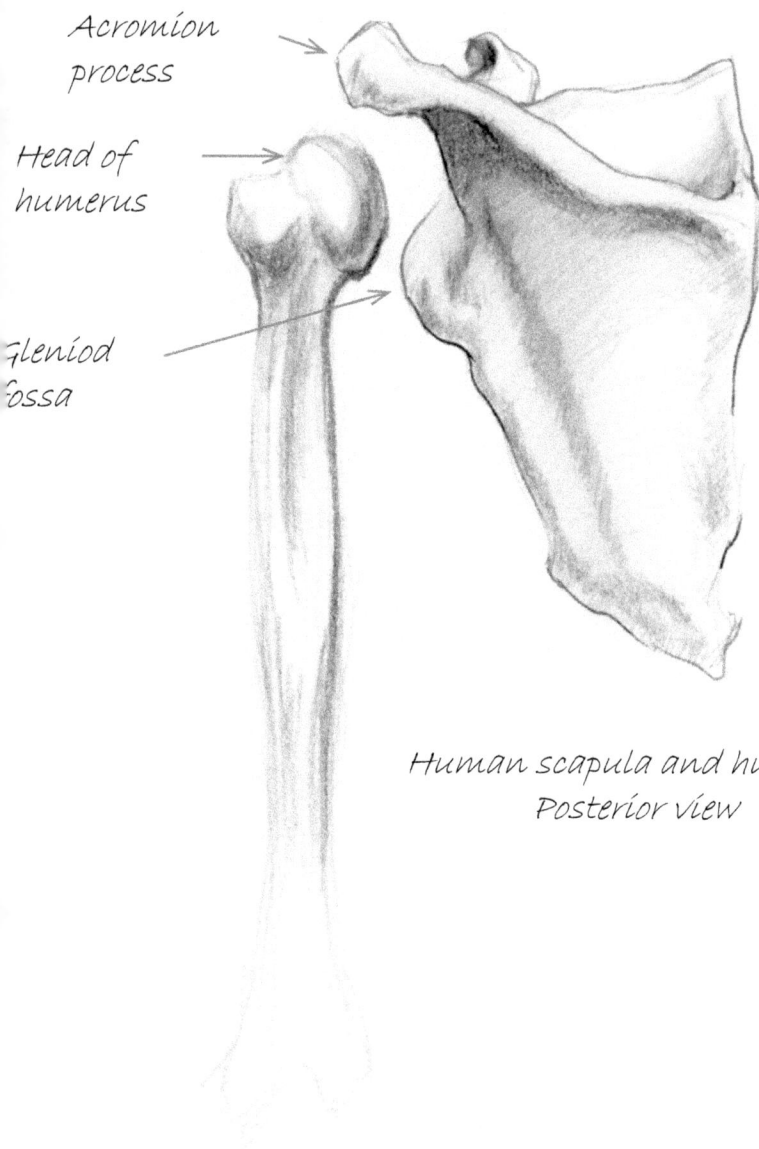

Human scapula and humerus
Posterior view

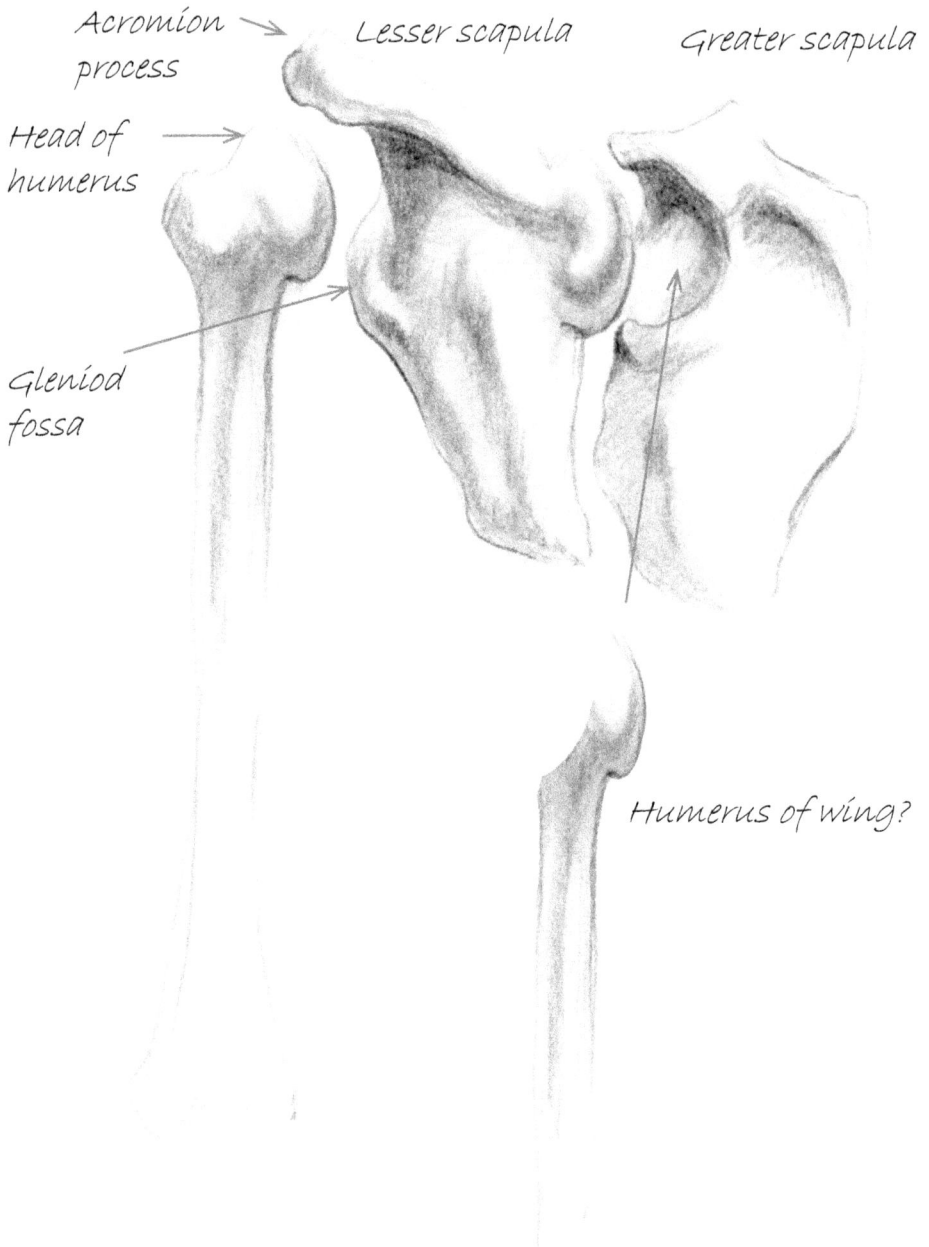

Acromion process

Lesser scapula

Greater scapula

Head of humerus

Gleniod fossa

Humerus of wing?

Vampire scapula and humeri
Posterior view

which would actually allow them to build a visual image in the brain from sound waves alone. This, though, is purely speculative and yet to be proven.

Unique Anatomical Feature

The scapula also shows distinct differences. The vampire scapula is split into two separate bones. The first is the minor scapula, which resembles that of a human and functions in a similar manner, allowing the arm the same range of movement as a human. It, however, is connected to the major scapula, which is absent in humans. Attachment is by means of a ball and socket joint, as found in the adjoining of the humerus to the scapula. The minor houses the head, which inserts into the fossa of the major scapula. This advancement in anatomy would give the vampire an almost equal horizontal range of posterior arm movement in addition to anterior usage. This posterior usage, however, is used solely for flight, and therefore, vertical movement of arms in reversed positions is limited.

Organs

Despite a digestive system specialized for their unique form of nourishment, vampires' organs are similar to those found in humans with one crucial difference: a double heart equidistant to the medial (positioned in the same position as the human heart but on both sides). Each measure approximately 5 by 2 inches, the same length as the human heart but approximately two-thirds the width. Each heart has two chambers, an atrium and a ventricle, which supply blood to one-half of the body. However, a shared vascular system is used. This means a counterclockwise circulation for the right-hand side and a clockwise circulation for the left-hand side so that opposing pressures are balanced. This important point dispels the superstition of vampires being killed by a stake through the heart. Two stakes would likely be required unless driven through from the side. However, since the use of a stake had the superstitious relevance of pinning a corpse to the earth, scientifically, as with any other creature, any implement puncturing the cardiac system would be fatal. One heart can probably sustain a vampire (unless there is heavy hemorrhaging); however, there would be a significant drop in blood pressure, causing poorer circulation and probable loss of energy unless an increased heart rate could be improvised.

8 - Days of Dusk and Dawn

On the fourth day, when the rains did break, I didn't hesitate but was back on the mountaintop at the first sign of clearing. I did take some more rope and a tarp to wrap the remains. I would attempt to move the creature with Petr's aid. I was anxious and fidgety upon returning, but after securing to the rock, I scaled the side without flinching in my excitement. However, upon reaching the spot, to my dismay, the remains were gone. For a moment I concluded I was simply in the wrong place, but with only one ledge, I soon found that such was not the case. The location was correct, which then made me hope the remains somehow had shifted with the rain. I crawled as deep as I could take myself into the hollow of the rock, but it was not there. It was dry further in, but only the faint smell of decomposition could still be smelt at the location it had laid in. Even though the rock was partially wet here, the odor was simply not strong enough anymore to suggest the corpse was still within the vicinity. Leaving the rope hanging over the edge with a white cloth, we hiked down and around to the base of the cliff. I was sure a flash flood of gushing water through the rock mass had exited the opening, thus lifting and pushing the corpse over the edge, but such was not the case either. I spent the whole morning searching in vain as my frustration grew, and then the afternoon brought rain again. This sent me into a brooding and pensive mood. This had to have been one of the greatest finds to date, but I had nothing to show for it other than notes, my word, and some small samples, which would surely be received with objection and suspicion. Who had moved the corpse, or better still, what had removed it? Could one of its own have found it? This was the only reasonable conclusion I could come to. I discounted another person finding it: its concealment and the treacherousness of the location during a dark rainstorm made it an impossible assumption. Petr and I combed the area for a week without finding a trace. He thought we were still looking for the boy.

Back in Bucegi, I was fixated by a spider in the window of the living room as it wrapped its prey in a waltz of silk. Pen in hand, I was trying to gather my thoughts, recording every detail of the event. Minor details I may have overlooked previously were now all important. Conjecture caused me to postulate the possibility of one of its own moving the corpse; if of higher intelligence, abstracts like death may touch them in ways similar to how it touches us. My train of thought was disrupted by the maid who entered to offer tea. The looseness in my grip caused my journal to slip, but my reactions were quick enough to catch it. However, a small white card made its exit to the

floor. Picking it up, I recalled the lady Ruxandra who had left it for me. I had almost forgotten about her, and so I inquired. The maid knew of her; everyone here did, it seemed, and she lived about an hour by carriage outside of the city on the slopes of the mountain. Almost for lack of motivation and my helpless disposition, I decided to pay her a visit. It would at least get my meandering mind off the events of the past week. That night, on August 8th, I penned Mr. Stefanistsa two letters, one a letter detailing in vague layman's prose the find, my loss, and my frustration, but without sounding like a madman. The second one was strictly scientific observation of the find and gave nothing other than the facts as I recalled them concerning the creature. Neither of these I signed, fearing some discredit to my reputation.

The following day a carriage brought me to the gates of what appeared to be a large estate, an estate that seemed out of place in such a rural area. There was an uneasiness in the horses. A large arched gate stood before us; one side of it opened, the other shut. The gates were no strangers to time, and rust had begun its feast long before my days, but the wrought iron seemed forged by time itself. Its design oozed and dripped as if the gate was melting or being pulled to the earth by a force greater than gravity. There had been an art style sweeping Europe towards the end of the last century, Art Nouveau, which blended Gothic with organics so that rounds and curves dressed its style. This was similar but older and not as uniform, deliberately done so. Before I knew it, the carriage was gone. The gates were supported by two pillars

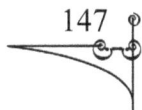

even more impressive in size, and likewise, their stone took a melting form. It reminded me of the styles I had seen in Barcelona some years earlier, but on a much grander scale; an oozing Gothic style was the best way to describe this seemingly amorphic structure. One would expect a wall on either side of the pillars, but strangely enough, there was none. The pillars became walls that tapered off like viscous wax rolling from a candle. The wildness of nature then became the wall; a fence of twisted vegetation, tall and lush with thorns, it crawled around the perimeter of the estate. Through the gate, I walked for what seemed to be an hour. A long pathway weaved through a private, misty sylvan, flanked by tall trees with smooth barks, foliaged at their tops only, joining long twining hands so that the sky was barely visible. There was a stillness here: no song of a bird, no buzz of a fly, just the rustling of leaves high above. The tree line eventually gave way to a clearing, which ran into another wooded area, and as I came into the clearing, a house became visible to my left. Large but unorthodox, it stood far taller than it was wide from my vantage point, but it was even larger in depth, disappearing beyond high walls and seemingly into the mountain behind it. Its construction again was strange. The walls and windows climbed into the sky like the steeples of a cathedral. The tall surrounding trees, mountains, and vast sky humbled its audacious presence so that its size fit the environs.

The door was a smooth, dark, polished material with rectangular colored glass inlaid in asymmetrical patterns. It opened by rolling into the

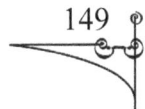

The Vampire 1897

wall like a huge wheel while the door itself remained
upright but not hinged like a regular door. It was
answered by a lady who I initially thought was
Ruxandra; she bore the same resemblance and exact
features but was much fairer in complexion and hair
color, strawberry blond hair with copper tones pulled
back and braided into an unusual, pointed bun that
rose before falling back from the crown of her head.
Her garb looked Asian in style, formfitting red silk
but with a black calligraphic pattern of pictograms
down the left side, which was both unusual and
eye-catching. I was greeted by name without even
having to introduce myself. She introduced herself as
Vishni and held out an elegant, slender hand, which
I kissed. From that point, she said nothing more
but brought me through one expanse after another
before leaving me in a room that had a sofa, a table,
and an unlit fireplace big enough that I could stand
up in it. As I waited, I felt dwarfed in the immense
room. No corners existed nor edges; everything was
rounded. The sparsely furnished, primitively somber
interiors opposed its grandiloquent Rococo potential.
The walls were like a smooth, grey stone but
untreated with paint or plaster. However, the relief
that decorated these walls was of a design foreign
to me, almost otherworldly, poured like secretions
from a resinous tree. Nothing was recognizable,
even the shapes, intricate and impregnated with
tiny grains that randomly sparkled. Its uniform
complexity assured me it was certainly made by the
hands of great artisans. I was feeling the bone-white
mantelpiece of the fireplace when a soft voice said,

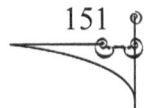

"Onyx." I would normally have jumped from the surprise, but her voice floated in harmony with the gentle draft running through the room. Ruxandra was standing next to me.

"You have a weightless stride—I didn't even hear you enter," I said. The room was large and empty, so I expected any sound to be amplified and echoed. I quickly corrected my casual chat.

"Excuse my manners, how are you, Ms…"

"Ruxandra. I'm fine," she replied within my hesitation.

I had been searching for a last name but recalled she had never left one. I felt awkward using a first name, so I inquired: "Is this usual amongst Romanian gentry to be addressed on a first-name basis, even by strangers?"

"You would have to ask Romanian gentry that question. First names are so much more personal, don't you think?" Her stare turned mechanically from me, and she walked to the sofa to sit.

Ruxandra was a paradox I had a hard time trying to figure out. Her demeanor, presence, and almost everything else about her was aristocratic to the highest level, but her laconic speech, though eloquent and educated, was casual beyond that of even friends. I sensed a liberty with her, a nonconforming liberty that was refreshing though baffling but made me feel completely comfortable around her. Vishni brought in coffee, and I was taken that coffee, not tea, was offered, and Ruxandra did not have any. Vishni, I learned, was Ruxandra's sister, which made sense: their likeness was striking.

However, I could not tell who was older and dared not ask. I figured it was Ruxandra, since Vishni had received and served me. I was also confused by the fact that a servant wasn't employed to perform this task. In fact, the house appeared void except for both sisters.

"You will dwell with us a few days I hope," Vishni said, in a manner I knew was rhetorical.

A nice bed and Ruxandra's magnetism alone wouldn't have met my refusal had it been a true question. I was not accustomed to such luxury nor attention, and though politeness should have prompted a well-mannered refusal, I felt Ruxandra's casualness in speech allowed me a similar acceptance. I was told not to worry about Petr. He would be cared for well in Bucegi, which really gave me no excuse.

In an attempt to be conversational, I remarked that the design style of the entrance to the estate had a similar construct to the entrance of Finca Miralles, for lack of a closer example in my naive knowledge of architecture. The residence, however, also exhibited medieval characteristics with Gothic influences. Ruxandra smiled and, looking at the walls, said, "These walls have stood for thousands of years, so perhaps it is this place that inspired Mr. Gaudi." I commented on how unusual the style was. Ruxandra replied in an almost defensive way, saying, "Think about it: what bird builds a square nest, or what bee a rectangular hive? The creatures of the earth build in harmony with it. There's a rhythm to nature that humans have missed. You build these angular, symmetrical structures that don't conform to nature's

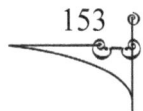

Batwoman 1890

way, so who is the unusual creature here?"

Her argument couldn't be refuted, and it opened my eyes to a unique richness she really had: her speech almost made her more empathetic with nature than with mankind. The way she addressed humankind almost indicated a separateness.

"I think it's very beautiful, just not something I've ever seen before," I answered in an apologetic tone. "So, when do I get a grand tour of your great abode?" I asked for lack of anything more insightful to say.

"Do you have a year?" she replied with a sarcastic smirk.

"That big," I said, assuming it was an exaggeration until she continued.

"The house goes back into the mountain and down, and it has chambers that not even I have been in. It eventually joins to the Krubera caves."

I had heard of these caves but didn't think they were near this area.

As we spoke, I began to realize that, although she was conversational, she never truly divulged anything about herself. She asked many questions and seemed to be familiar with what I was doing in Bucegi. Her questions were often pointed and too detailed for her not to know the answer herself; perhaps she was testing my honesty. I also found out that Mr. Stefanistsa was known to her, which made sense and explained how she had known me in Bucharest. I began to sense that I was, in some way, part of an esoteric circle, or at least a guest to it, if not an acolyte. Their interest and knowledge

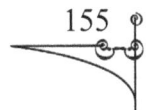

of recent events were surreal but too connected to be coincidence. At times I noticed there was an emptiness in her eyes, distancing her.

After some time, I was shown to the dimly lit dining room and left alone to dine while she politely took her leave. The table I sat at was large and amoeba-shaped, with a huge hole in its center. Long, thin, cone-like tubulous structures rose through the center, winding upwards and terminating at different heights one to five feet above the table, all aflame. Upon leaning forward I caught no glimpse of any wick or candle. They appeared hollow, fueled perhaps by a gas or a liquid. The backless seats took on the contours of the table, each one different and customized to the lay of the table. Their firm, comfortable cushions looked as if they were made from a natural sponge set within a transparent, pliable resin. I ate a delectable meal of rare, tender meats and vegetables. My palate was then cleansed with the choicest wine, which was served from a crystal decanter, which rose like a twisted teardrop, hand cut so that it refracted sparkles from the flame.

No sooner had I finished than Ruxandra appeared again and led me to a great hallway, where a conch-like sweeping staircase wound into the high air above. The stairs were of a grey stone like the walls, but the banisters were a marbled white carved onyx. I was told where my room was and informed that should I get lost or confused, it was the only door unlocked. Vishni now entered from a room I had not seen, embraced Ruxandra at the waist, and kissed her tenderly on the left cheek before nudging her

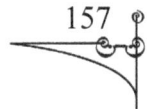

forehead against Ruxandra's temple and dropping it on her shoulder, where she again kissed her gently on the neck. In saying good night to Ruxandra, she stared intently at me while still embracing her at the waist. They spoke a few words in a foreign language that I knew was not Romanian simply based on its phonetics and inflections. It wasn't until Ruxandra returned Vishni a kiss on the forehead that her embrace loosened, and she was excused to go. She slipped out of the hallway soundlessly and was gone. We remained a few moments extra and talked before Ruxandra pointed out the obvious: that my eyes were heavy and in need of rest. She reminded me about locking my door at night.

  I found my room as directed. The bed was the largest one I had ever slept in and wasn't a conventional one. It came out of the wall and was part of it, not freestanding nor touching the floor. Wide and low, it seemed to float, and as soon as I lay on it, I was fast asleep. The following morning, I awoke well rested and what I thought was too early. No clocks existed in the room, nor anywhere else in the house, for that matter. I noticed some light seeping in through a small kidney-shaped window high above my head, so I knew it wasn't too early. As I splashed running water on my face from a black circular basin that seemed suspended in air, it dawned on me that most of the house lay in twilight. Windows sat very high on the walls, too high to be viewed through but too small to ever allow light to strike the floor. Light was always funneled onto the walls, where some reflection occurred, but the greyness of the stone captured much of its strength. The upwards expanse was greater in each room than its breadth or depth. The only two larger windows I had noticed when entering were long and thin in the shape of flames, made with a densely stained glass through which a kaleidoscope of dappled colors danced on the floors, choreographed by the movement of foliage from outside trees, but even these windows, which stretched some thirty feet high, had long, velvet opaque curtains that could be drawn, offering an opacity close to stone.

Breakfast was laid out, accompanied by a short note indicating the location of the library. I was also told that if walking outside, I was not to go beyond the walls that extended on either side of the house. I took a pleasant stroll on the grounds that morning. I felt relaxed with a slight breeze on my face and in the warmth of a low-sitting sun. After clambering up slippery slopes, I walked along the walls that ran along both sides of the house and was able to peer through a tall, locked gate, practically impervious to sight from the thick growth it latticed. The garden on the other side ran wild and unkept and was shaded by the daunting height of the house on one side, trees on the other, and the mountains behind. The end of the house didn't appear to have a rear wall but was swallowed into the mountain slope, which rose steeply behind. It looked as if the mountain had been poured behind it and had enveloped it as liquid mud would a stone. Quite a feat of engineering, if indeed the house did go further back into the mountain.

Later that morning, I took a seat in the

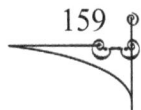

impressive library, more impressive than the one at Mr. Stefanistsa's manor in County Meath. Its shelves were solid cutouts in the wall. Much of the library contained books in foreign languages and from far-off places such as the Orient, their ages spanning centuries. An ornate Egyptian book caught my attention. Its papyrus pages made it thick, and its partial gold and silver binding made it loud, standing out boldly from the drab and aged leather-bound ones sandwiching it. Pulling it off the shelf, I turned, only to jump back. Ruxandra, standing right before me, smiled apologetically. She led me to the circular couch, which was sunken into the floor, six steps deep to the split level, which broke the couch from being a complete circle.

"12th century," she said.

"Really!" I said, surprised and without another word to find.

"When Egypt was beginning to wane," she continued.

I put the book gently down. I thought she had referred to the 12th century on this side of Christ, but when I saw it was on the other side, I was taken.

"But it's in codex form!" I exclaimed.

"There are many mistakes your kind has not yet realized," she replied.

Again, as before, her use of the word "kind" perplexed me.

"Such valuable antiquity shouldn't be handled," I said, but she returned to her casual self, reassuring me it was just a book, though a beautifully illustrated one. We talked a bit, and then she was gone again. It was an isolating day but refreshing. I saw Ruxandra only twice, for an hour or so each

meeting, but did not see Vishni at all. I was growing fond of Ruxandra's company, though perhaps her strange charm was an active ingredient in that fondness.

My day dissolved rather quickly in the library with my insatiable appetite for books. Part of my time there, I pondered on a strange conversation I had had with Ruxandra earlier. She had begun the conversation by asking,

"So tell me, do you now believe in vampires?"

"You know of my find then," I had replied, staring directly at her, wide-eyed.

"I know many things."

"Do you know what happened to the remains?" I excitedly inquired.

"Yes, but you have seen enough for now," she said while glancing directly at me with a gaze that penetrated to the marrow. I felt a shiver run through me. I sensed there was a connection between her and the creature. I didn't dare push the issue any further. If she had allowed me the privilege of discovering this magnificent creature, I would be grateful. By now I felt she would divulge more information in time. She then changed the subject and, over the course of an hour, asked what I knew about hybrids, mutations, speciation, and interbreeding.

My reply was that these areas of science were in their infancy. Species that are extremely close do have the potential for interbreeding, but sterility results, and there are also other complexities to consider, such as gestation periods, etc.

"What about pathogens of the blood?" she asked.

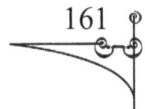

"Again, we are only beginning to explore the workings of our own bodies. Why?" I asked, feeling an emptiness within her.

Ruxandra ended the conversation by looking straight ahead and saying, "Perhaps it is not yet time. I shall have to wait a little longer." She then excused herself.

I got the distinct feeling she had half-expected my answers but had hoped for more. I was nonetheless surprised by her strange questions. What did she mean by "the time is not right"?

Time was hard to gauge in the house; my watch had also stopped ticking. The little external light that existed was hard to follow; nonetheless, illumination within the rooms seemed to be self-regulating. The lack of translucency in the stained glass indicated night and signaled bedtime again. I had climbed about twenty stairs or so when Ruxandra bid me good night from the bottom and apologized for her absence. I replied that her collection of books had been more than enough company and thanked her again for her extended hospitality.

I awoke at some point during the night, not due to any external interference — I simply woke. The room was a series of black and charcoal blotches. The undulating surface of the walls created blurred and even blacker shadows within the blackness of the night. No moon nor star was visible, and without any large window, very little stray night light had made its way in. I was turning to close my eyes again when I sensed movement in the furthest corner of the room, which stopped as quickly as my eye had caught it. I strained to see, but nothing took any shape other than

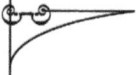

the fluid shapes already within the room's design. My eyes closed again, and my conscious mind began to slip when I felt a weighted presence at the bottom corner of the bed, next to my right foot. It was subtle, but the linen beneath my foot pulled slightly from it. As a result, I raised my head only to see a form taking shape. I now fully realized the movement of something on the bed on both sides of me. Before I could even raise myself in fright, it was above me.

"Ruxandra? Vishni?" I whispered in a gasping confusion.

She didn't speak but smiled. Her hair was loosened and wild, copiously long, sultry, dark hair that I had only seen pulled back in her diurnal presence. Her large, dark eyes were lit with flame and reflected a silver sheen though no light in the room could be seen. I was partially frozen by the shock of it all but overcome and calmed by the scent of jasmine that only seemed to trail her in the evening. I fell back into the bed, and she lowered herself to kiss me gently on the lips before running her tongue meticulously up and down my neck. Her luxuriant, perfumed hair fell onto my face and neck, its soft, supple weight like wispy, fragrant fingers moving in gyrations across my skin before she rose up to stare at me again. I began to talk, but no sooner had I opened my mouth than she sealed it with a strong finger pressed to my lips. Her dark, silken undergarment revealed the contours of her curvaceous form beneath. Glimmering slightly, it fell loosely around her body like a secondary skin. Taking my hands, she placed them firmly on her breasts, which I started fondling nervously. Then, clenching my wrists, she pressed them down onto the

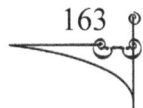

pillow behind my head as she assumed her previous position on all fours. Moving her body forwards and downwards, she began toying with me, kissing and nibbling. She released my hands, and they moved around her back and slid onto her hips. Slowly, they continued down to her outer thighs and under her silk gown, then to her underbelly with stretched thumbs before cautiously finding their way to her warm inner thighs. Scouting with fingertips, she was testing my boldness as to how far I would go or, should I say, she would allow me to go. At the top of her inner thighs, as I approached warm, moist boundaries, she arched her back like a threatened cat, pulling abruptly away from me. Her hands grabbed and tightened on my wrists again, and I was held against the bed as the insteps of her feet slid down my shins, clamping my ankles like hands in a cuffed fashion. I struggled to free myself, not out of fear, but under the assumption she was still toying. I quickly realized her strength was far superior to mine — it was as if I had four men pinning me down, one on each limb. I felt a chill sweep my body. Her eyes were now lively and seemed to dance as she scanned areas of my exposed torso but with a distant, foreign stare. She then again made eye contact and smiled. For a moment, I thought I had lost her, but she seemed to return in the smile.

She stooped to kiss me again on the lips, and the tension in my body subsided in submission to her advances. I closed my eyes as she spent time kissing and nudging my neck with her nose when I felt a sharp pinprick. My body jumped, stretching and becoming rigid, with my midsection flexing

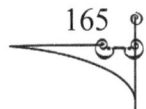

upwards as my muscles contracted but without any peripheral freedom as I was still pinned. I initially felt a discomfort, a heat that surged through my body accompanied by a nauseous feeling which dispersed and was followed by the sensation of flowing fluid due to a temperature differential in my neck causing it to stiffen. The vixen appeared lifeless; there was no movement in her, but her grip on me was still stone solid. I began feeling claustrophobic, like I was pinned beneath a huge rock, unable to breathe, weakening by the second. I lost consciousness a short time later.

The following morning I awoke with a dull headache. On opening my eyes, I found the room as normal as it was the night before. I felt fatigued and woozy and thus assumed I was coming down with something. My sheets were clean. With no mirrors around, I couldn't check my neck, but it felt fine. Was last night a bad dream or the return of those feverish hallucinogenic bouts of my youth? Unlocking my door to go downstairs confirmed it was all in my head. Vishni served me breakfast that morning, and I related how I had missed seeing her yesterday. She received the compliment with a smile and a slight bow of the head, without word and without eye contact. My neck felt stiff, but I assumed it was psychosomatic from the dream or perhaps due to sleeping in an unusual position. I was rubbing my neck and relating my dream to Vishni when she came behind me and gently massaged my neck. Her hands and warm body pressed against my back revived the dream. Ruxandra was now seeping into my thoughts, and I longed to see her that day.

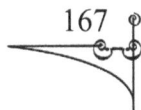

The day came and went with me slipping in and out of sleep as I attempted to read in the library. Over the course of the next week, I awoke each morning feeling fatigued, sometimes incoherent. I did not see Ruxandra during the course of this time but often had fragmented relapses of the initial hallucination. With only Vishni around, her presence substituted somewhat, though she lacked Ruxandra's forward, confident charm. I would often feel her close to me with caring and caressing touches, but I sensed a nervousness that always interrupted her otherwise relaxing touch. Even with the feeling of her soft, soothing hands on my shoulders and in her care, I was not getting any better. Cold sweats began accompanying my bouts of delirium.

At some point, I was fetched from the house and taken all the way back through Europe without much recollection of the journey. I faintly recall staying at various houses, similar kinds of houses but with different layouts. It seemed perpetually dark to me, like we traveled by night.

The decision to leave Ruxandra's abode was not mine; I was hardly in the best health to make it, and even if I was well, I would have been reluctant to do so. Someone else had made the decision. I don't recall much of the end of my trip and don't remember my journey back to Dublin nor the last few months here in hospital. I have spent the last few days sorting through mail and compiling this journal. I have walked the grey corridors of my mind, pulling data from shuffled, disarrayed bookshelves that stretch around blind corners in an effort to sort the tangible from the intangible, and there have been

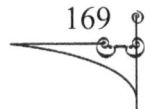

times when I even thought this journal was a figment of my imagination. It felt like flu season all over again, but a prolonged, amplified one. A letter from Petr assured me he had gotten home safely. I had been worried about him. I replied with an apology to his parents and him. While in hospital, I received a card from Mr. Stefanistsa, hoping for my well-being. Payment for services also accompanied the letter, but he said nothing about the details concerning the find, which I had mailed to him, and so his letter left me wondering. Other aids, too becoming for such an ordinary man, were also at work.

Rain and the grey winter months back in Dublin brought a certain nostalgia for the place I had spent such a short time in. The more I thought about the nocturnal visitations from my gorgeous succubus, the more I felt connected to her. My brief time in Romania had been an eventful one, to say the least: part pleasurable, part frightening, though provocatively strange and dismayed. I had encountered two strange creatures, the beautiful Ruxandra and the creature I found on a cliff's edge. Were these two separate creatures or the two faces of an ingenious one, one far higher on the ladder of life than we ourselves? If there was a connection between these two creatures, one thing was common: both were female, and therefore it was possibly a matriarchal family or genus.

It was now approaching December again. My post had been restored and secured back at Trinity College by what I felt was a power beyond me, as I hardly had the tenure or brilliance to warrant such

security. I would resume teaching in January. Now at home, I was still under physician care, the type only afforded by the wealthy, but such payment wasn't coming from my pocket. A day nurse and a night nurse tended to me at intervals around the clock. It was not uncommon for them to change shifts without my knowledge and at irregular scheduling times throughout the course of the week, details I wasn't concerned about. Nurses also rotated, and just as I was getting used to one, another would take her place.

Though feeling much more back to normal, I still had dizzy spells and bouts of fevers. My sight was often dark and blurred, while at other times, I saw with pristine sharpness. One evening a week prior to Christmas, I awoke from a nightmare in the dark hours of the morning. In a cold sweat with a raised head, I gasped, but with the faint light through a familiar window, I eased back onto the pillow.

The nurse tending me wiped my forehead with a cloth, pacifying me solely with the comfort of her conscious presence. She spoke no words and gently wiped my face, and her index and middle finger stroked the length of my neck. I was beginning to relax and drift when a sweetness filled my nostrils, and a lock of golden hair fell onto my face as a moist, full pair of lips kissed my right cheek with hyper-sensual familiarity. Aroused, I stirred my mind, trying to focus on the blurred vision before me. I couldn't see anything but a warm silhouette when the scent of jasmine and moonflower bloomed and enveloped a catatonically seduced me.

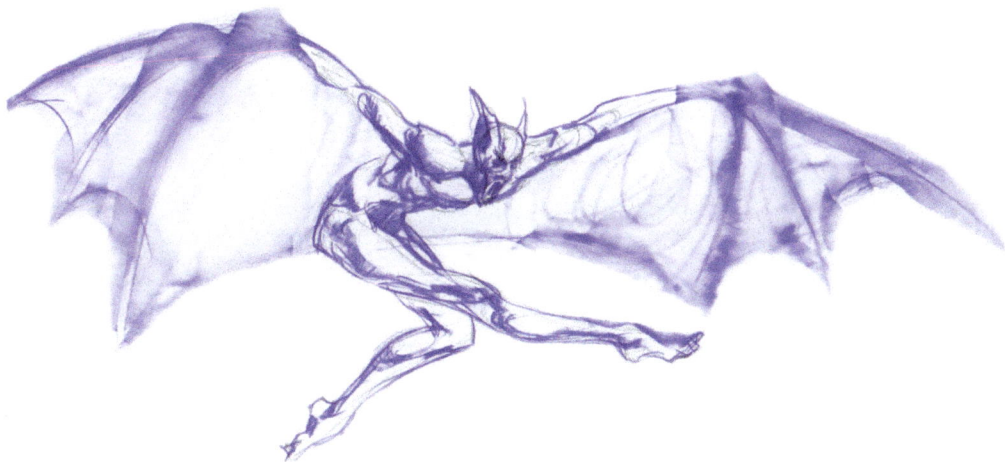

Memories of Mist

Neighb'ring sylvan shone a light
Warm and glowing elusive sprite
More yellow than the moon
Far fainter than the sun
From my room I watched it move
In a swirling, aery dance of muse
falling silver leaf from bough on high
Beneath still night in autumn sky

Approached I did in caution still
Wild eyes stared from darkness deep
none dared enter a dryads light
she brought me in, rapt by sight
Pale flesh of hers in see through white
She stared and stunned then
whispered right, a bold invite
I am yours and you are mine
Here drink these ruby waters fine,
From the navel of Dionysus
Held by hip, entwined by vine

Both lips partake and shared in sip
bound we'll be, in silk scarfs of time

Fabled Fand in woods grown real
Song and mirth, provoking flirt
embraced the night until fell'd from flight
When I awoke on moss draped quilt
Stripped beneath denuded sky.
Stains off vintage upon skin and palms
were it had leaked from a vessel shared
but no such wine could pain me more
a neck love bit but deeper sore

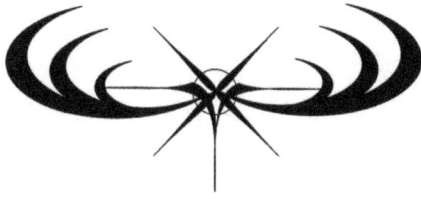

VAMPIRE (dictionary definition)

A bat of the family Desmodontidae.

A reanimated corpse that is believed to rise from
the grave at night to suck the blood of sleeping
people.

A person or living organism who preys upon other life.

A woman who exploits and ruins her lover.

New entry?

Until we observe them in nature, capture or others
also find the corporeal remains of this creature, I will
never be believed. Will we ever truly know of their
existence or will these creatures forever haunt our
imaginations and remain as obscure as the nights they
roam.

Dr. A Lucard

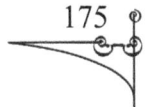

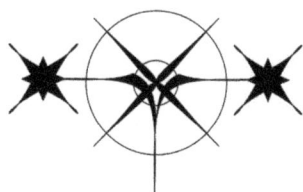

The exact roots of the word vampire are as vague as the true origins of the creature itself. Vampire comes from German *Vampir*, in turn from early Old Polish *vąper* (where ą is a nasal a, and both p and r' are palatalized), in turn from Old Slavic *oper (with a nasal o) or Old Church Slavonic *opiri*. It is similar to Serbian verb *piriti*, "to swell", and to Greek *apyros*, "not undergone by fire." The Slavic word, like its cognate *netopyr'* ("bat"), comes from the "PIE" root for "to fly." While other sources cite the Slavic languages of Eastern Europe in the Middle Ages where the word is found in abundance. Russian, Polish, Czech, Bulgarian, and Serbo-Croatian all had *vampir*, while Bulgarian also had *vapir* or *vepir*. There is also a variant beginning with u, as in Polish *upiór*, Russian *upyr'*, and Ukrainian *uper* or *upyr*. It is possible that this u-word came from Turkish *uber*, meaning "witch," and also possible that the u-word spelling was the ancestor of vampire.

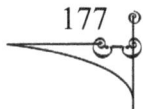

Images And Citations:

pxi Fantaisie Egyptienne by Charles Allen Winter 1898
p20 The Illustrated London News Front Page Title block 1842
p23 - 25 Akkadian seal, Burney Relief and early map of Babylon.
p30 Lilith by John Collier 1892
p34 Lamia by Herbert Draper 1909
p41 Excerpts from Christabel (1797-1800) by Samuel Taylor Coleridge
p44 Excerpts from Carmilla 1872 by J Sheridan LeFanu
p54 Woodcut by Ambrosius Huber 1499
p58 Vlad the Impaler and the Turkish envoy, Theodor Aman, c. 1880
p150 The Vampire by Philip Burne-Jones 1897
p154 Batwoman by Albert Penot 1890
p173 Memories of Mist, anonymous

Note:
p49 Conceptual Crest (Actual crest likely a prostrated dragon)

Anatomy of a Vampire, the Series

Anatomy of a Vampire 1912 is the first part of a series laying a foundation for the next installment, which is set in the present. Beyond that, the series will move into the future before going back in time to their earthly beginning.

About the Author

Author John Matthias, a native of Ireland, ventured abroad in search of sunnier climes and a more fulfilling life. His travels led him to the United States where he met his gorgeous wife, a fellow artist. They settled in a bright corner of the country and began a family. John is a writer and illustrator by trade. When not at work in the technology sector, he enjoys spending quality time with family and friends, accompanied by a craft brew or a cup of boutique coffee. He enjoys reading, film, art, and home improvement projects.

9 798822 966581